Frank Warren Hackett

A Sketch of the Life and Public Services of William Adams Richardson

Frank Warren Hackett

A Sketch of the Life and Public Services of William Adams Richardson

ISBN/EAN: 9783337009649

Printed in Europe, USA, Canada, Australia, Japan

Cover: Foto ©Raphael Reischuk / pixelio.de

More available books at **www.hansebooks.com**

Richardson, William Adams; a Sketch of the Life and Public Services of — by Frank Warren Hackett: Washington, 1898.

William A. Richardson

A SKETCH OF THE LIFE AND PUBLIC SERVICES

OF

WILLIAM ADAMS RICHARDSON

BY

FRANK WARREN HACKETT

Privately Printed

WASHINGTON

1898

Press of H. L. McQueen,
Washington.

CONTENTS.

———

III. INDEX OF NAMES.

To the Reader.

It was my good fortune to make the acquaintance of William Adams Richardson upwards of thirty years ago, when both of us were living at Cambridge, Massachusetts. He was then judge of probate and insolvency for Middlesex county, while I had but recently opened a law office in Boston. For a brief season we met daily at the table of the famous boarding house kept by Miss Upham, on Kirkland street, near the college.

Early in 1873 my removal to Washington, where I have ever since practiced my profession, afforded me an opportunity, which I was glad to improve, of continuing our acquaintance. Though his junior by many years, I was honored by being to a certain extent admitted to the confidence of his friendship. The better I came to know the man, the more highly I esteemed him.

Shortly after Judge Richardson's death one of the executors of his will placed in my hands a letter addressed to myself. The Judge had written it without date. In modest terms he had expressed a wish that I might prepare a sketch of his life, to be printed and copies distributed to friends, and to various public libraries. This office I have cheerfully accepted, solicitous only that his true proportions may be made to appear, and the leading features of his important public service be adequately set forth.

Upon the whole record of his achievements I am of the deliberate conviction that Richardson was an abler and a more valuable public official than has been commonly supposed. The reader who shall peruse the narrative — particularly if he weigh the testimony of the bar and of the court given in the proceedings as printed in the Appendix — is already in a fair way, I believe, to reach a like conclusion.

Judge Richardson loved the truth, and despised anything that savored of pretense. I have tried to tell a plain, straightforward story of his remarkably useful life, knowing that he himself would have wished the facts,—precisely as they occurred,—presented with simplicity and candor.

FRANK WARREN HACKETT.

CRAIGHFEN,
  NEW CASTLE, NEW HAMPSHIRE,
    20 September, 1898.

SKETCH OF LIFE

WILLIAM ADAMS RICHARDSON.

Of THE tier of towns that stretch along the New Hampshire line, in Middlesex County, Massachusetts, all of them attractive in the season of summer, none is fairer than little Tyngsborough. With fields well tilled and comfortable dwellings, pleasantly shaded, her territory, cut in two as it is by the broad and placid stream of the Merrimack, presents to the traveller at well-nigh every turn a picture of rural delight.

She has the name of Tyngsborough all to herself. Not another spot on the globe is so entitled. A part of "Dunstable Plantation" it used to be, when land was cheaper and towns bigger. One Edward Tyng, it seems, born in the mother country, about 1600, had married Mary Sears, who, tradition says, came from Dunstable, England. He emigrated to Boston where he rose to be a person of consequence, after which, stimulated by your true Englishman's craving for broad acres, he spied out a tract of some three or four thousand overlooking the Merrimack at this beautiful site, and made it his own. Hither he removed and had descendants. "Dunstable" is said to have been named in 1673 in compliment to Mistress Mary Tyng; while it was left to later somebodies to bestow the oddity of the surname upon the modest borough carved out of a grander domain.*

As in duty bound her local historian sounds Tyngsborough's praises, the starting place, he tells us, of boys who grew to be distinguished; and, truth to say, for so small a place there has been a deal of happening there that the world ought more or less to keep in mind, notably in the way of births.

Among these who going out of this quiet town have gained worldly success and honors, no one has reached higher distinction than WILLIAM ADAMS RICHARDSON, born at Tyngsborough, 2 November, 1821, who became Secretary of the Treasury; and who, when he died at Washington, 19 October, 1896, was Chief Justice of the Court of Claims of the United States.

The writer is about to attempt to outline the main features of the busy and exceptionably useful life of this eminent public servant, well

---

*"Their great-grand-daughter, Madam Sarah Tyng Winslow, nearly a century and a quarter later, became the benefactress of a portion of the plantation, and in honor of her family name the new town in 1809 was christened Tyngsborough." *MS. letter of J. Franklin Bancroft, of Tyngsborough*, 30 August, 1898.

aware that perhaps little more need be done than to recount the numerous stations of trust and responsibility to which, one after another, he was summoned, and tell without embellishment with what measure of fidelity he filled each of them in turn.

It may be said of William Adams Richardson that he was fortunate of descent. He could carry up his line through generations of strong and worthy ancestors of English breeding; men whose highest aim it was to live a useful life. The earliest known progenitor on the father's side was Ezekiel Richardson, who, with his wife Susanna, became a member of the church gathered at Charlestown, in Massachusetts Bay, 27 August, 1630. As yet it has not come to light from what part of the kingdom Ezekiel Richardson emigrated, but the conjecture is not altogether without foundation that his home was in one of the southern counties. There is in fact scant room for doubt that the ship which brought him to these shores was one of the fleet bringing over the company under the leadership of Winthrop, in the spring of 1630. It is of record that Ezekiel Richardson was admitted as a freeman 18 May, 1631.

Sundry entries in the records of Charlestown testify that Ezekiel Richardson must have been a man of more than ordinary capacity. His

landed possessions, as recorded in 1638, were
extensive; in fact, he ranks among the largest
owners, while his brothers Samuel and Thomas
follow close upon him in the same year, their
holdings being of nearly as many acres.* The
general court appointed him constable at
Charlestown in 1633. Later he was chosen
selectman, and sent as a deputy to the general
court.

The most noteworthy entry in the colony
records referring to the Richardsons is that telling of his attitude towards the Reverend John
Wheelwright, the faithful and zealous minister,
who afterwards left Massachusetts and founded
Exeter, in New Hampshire. This godly man
was a connection by marriage of Mistress Anne
Hutchinson. The religious views of Mistress
Hutchinson, it will be remembered, threw the
community of Boston Bay into agitation ; and in
the controversy that fiercely raged over the doctrine of antinomianism Wheelwright did not
hesitate to take sides with her. These views
were in reality approved by a large proportion of
the members of the Boston church, though the
Puritan authorities held them in abhorrence.
With unsparing rigor the general court caused
to be made known its disapproval of such sedi-

---

* *Report of Record Commissioners containing Charlestown land records*
1638-1802 (2nd edition) Boston, 1883—pp. 3, 4, and 5.

tious teachings as that of Mistress Hutchinson; and straightway passed sentence upon the clergyman who had lent support to her obnoxious sentiments.

The current of popular feeling, however, set strongly in Wheelwright's favor, and many of the best people, as well as "the humblest artisans and day-laborers," hastened to come forward and sign their names to a petition of remonstrance in his behalf. This occurred in March, 1637. The names of the remonstrants are preserved. Ten persons likewise are designated upon the record, who having subscribed the document had later the comfort of seeing their names erased "on acknowledgment of their sin in subscribing it." Among the ten names we find that of Ezekiel Richardson, who thus escaped being disarmed; to say nothing of other and worse penalties which a facing of the disapproval of the magistrates would have brought upon him. A modern writer remarks, naively enough, of Ezekiel Richardson's conduct: "It is creditable to his memory that he was willing to abandon an enterprise in which he had conscientiously but unwisely embarked."*

The two younger brothers just mentioned, Samuel and Thomas, it is thought came to New

---

* *The Richardson Memorial, by John Adams Vinton,* (Portland, 1876) p. 33—a genealogical work to which the present writer is much indebted.

England in 1636, six years later than Ezekiel. We find the record of land assigned to the three brothers 30 April, 1637, on " Misticke side and above the Pond," that is to say, in what is now Malden. Four years afterward (1641) the three Richardsons, in company with six other persons, founded the town of Woburn, not far from Charlestown. The brothers lived near each other in the same street, which, because it had been continuously occupied by their posterity for years, long since gained the name of " Richardson's Row." The row formed a portion of Washington street in what is now the town of Winchester. Ezekiel Richardson played a conspicuous part in the public affairs of the community he had helped to establish. He was named, with two others (who were deacons in the church) " to end small causes under twenty shillings."

After a life of much stir and activity, though apparently not prolonged beyond five and forty years, he died at Woburn, 21 October, 1647. His will is on file in Boston. The inventory of his estate amounts to a total of one hundred and ninety pounds.

The second son of Ezekiel and Susanna Richardson was Josiah, baptized at Charlestown, 7 November, 1635. He was married June, 1659, at Concord, to Remembrance Underwood of that town. He thereupon removed with his brother

James to Chelmsford, a town pleasantly seated on the south side of the Merrimack. Here Josiah Richardson promptly came to the front as a man of enterprise and a leading citizen. Joining with two others he built the first saw-mill of the town. He was chosen constable and town clerk, as well as selectman; and the military company elected him captain, no empty honor in those days of threatened trouble with a savage foe. From the record in the Middlesex county registry of a conveyance executed by two of Eliot's Indians, dated 19 January, 1688, we learn that Captain Josiah Richardson once owned that portion of the territory on which now stand nearly all of the large manufactories of the city of Lowell. It may not be advisable for us at this late date to probe too deeply into the nature of the consideration recited as supporting this deed. According to the language of the record, the Indians conveyed the land for " ye love we bear for ye beforesaid Josiah."

This latter ancestor had an elder son, also of the name of Josiah, who was born at Chelmsford, 18 May, 1665. He likewise attained to military honors, enjoying the title of lieutenant. On 14 December, 1687, Josiah Richardson married Mercy Parish of Dunstable, a town at that time in Massachusetts, now Nashua in New Hampshire. Though not advanced to so many or so high honors as his father, Lieutenant Josiah appears to have reached a prominence in public affairs somewhat similar to that of both father and grandfather. He was called by the people of Chelmsford to the office of selectman, and likewise to that of town clerk. He led the quiet life of a farmer near Concord river. He appears to have been fairly well provided with what in those days must have proved a prime requisite for carrying on a farm,—namely, children. According to the records, Josiah and Mercy Richardson were blessed with four sons and two daughters, all born at Chelmsford. Of these the youngest, William, first saw the light of day 19 September, 1701.

It was the fortune of William Richardson to carry on a farm, like his ancestors. Upon reaching the age of twenty-one, he was married to Elizabeth Colburn, of Dracut, a town near the present city of Lowell. He settled in what later became Pelham, New Hampshire, which territory having originally formed a portion of the town of Dracut, in Massachusetts, found itself in 1741 across the line as a part of another state. Pelham was incorporated as a town in 1746, and in 1751 had its meeting house, and a minister to whom was voted, in addition to his salary, "twenty-five cords of fire-wood annually."

Here William Richardson passed an uneventful

life, except that there fell to him the family inheritance of a military title, for he served as captain in the militia for many years. The people of Pelham sent him to represent them in the general court. He lived to a good, old age, long enough, in fact, to have heard the opening guns of the Revolution. His death occurred at Pelham some time later than the early part of 1776; his will dated the 1st of April that year, having been proved on the 7th of November following. William and Elizabeth Richardson had nine children, the youngest of whom was Daniel, born in Pelham, 1749. He was the grandfather of the subject of this sketch.

Arrangements appear to have been made to confer upon Daniel Richardson the advantages of a college education. To this end his father sent him to Dracut (not far, to be sure) in order that he might recite Latin to the Reverend Mr. Davis of that town. How faithfully the young man pursued his studies we are not informed, but he improved the opportunity there, it seems, to fall in love with Sarah Merchant,* a daughter of William Merchant of Boston. Mrs. Merchant, her mother, was Abigail Hutchinson, a sister of Governor Hutchinson. Miss Merchant favored her

---

*Sarah Merchant was the oldest of several orphan children. Care of her had been committed to her uncle, Mr. Dennie, of Boston, a brother of her mother. Being a single man, he sent Sarah at the age of eighteen to board and be educated with the family of Reverend Mr. Davis of Dracut. Mrs. Richardson is said to have been a woman of great ability and energy.

suitor, and the result was an early marriage, on 26 January, 1773. Their union had the effect to change entirely the course of Daniel Richardson's life, for instead of going to college, he betook himself to tilling the soil, living in Pelham on a farm, a part of which belonged to his father.

Daniel, as might be expected, had inherited the Richardson taste for military service. In those stirring times, it was not uncommon for the farmer to be transformed at short notice into the soldier. Daniel Richardson shouldered his musket, and did his share of service in the revolutionary war. He enlisted 1 January, 1777, in the First New Hampshire Regiment, Colonel Joseph Cilley, and served until 5 January, 1780.* Mention is made of his having fought in the battle of Monmouth, 28 June, 1778. In the following summer he was of the expedition led by General Sullivan into the Indian country, in the western part of the state of New York. Upon returning home he became captain of a military company in New Hampshire.

Everything that we learn of Daniel Richardson stamps him as a man of firm character, and worthy of the marked respect in which he appears to have been held by his neighbors. He lived to the ripe age of eighty-four, and died at

---

* *History of the First New Hampshire Regiment in the War of the Revolution, by Frederick Kidder,* Albany, 1868.

Pelham 23 May, 1833. His children were three sons, all born in Pelham; William Merchant, born 4 January, 1774; Samuel Mather, born 12 February, 1776; Daniel, born 19 January, 1783.

Of these sons the eldest, William Merchant Richardson, achieved an honorable distinction as chief justice of New Hampshire. He was graduated from Harvard College, in the class of 1797, with Horace Binney, Daniel Appleton White and John Collins Warren as classmates. For a season he was preceptor at Groton Academy. Studying law with Samuel Dana, of Groton, he later became a partner of that distinguished man. The people sent Mr. Richardson as representative to Congress from the Groton district in 1811, to fill a vacancy. He shortly afterwards resigned his seat in Congress and removed to New Hampshire, where he was made United States attorney, with his office at Portsmouth. Such remarkable ability did he display from the beginning that on the reorganization of the courts in 1816, Governor Plumer sent in his name to be chief justice of the highest court of the state, and he was unanimously confirmed, in spite of the intensity with which party spirit raged at that season. This high office Chief Justice Richardson filled until his death, for a period of twenty-two years, to the great satisfaction of the bar and the people of the state.

When the new chief justice came to the bench, there were no published reports of adjudicated cases. He at once set about to remedy the defect. He introduced a number of improvements in the methods of practice. To the end that stability and harmony might be insured in the administration of inferior judicial offices, he prepared manuals respectively for justices of the peace, sheriffs and town officers, containing all needful forms and directions. In a word, the chief justice to the last proved himself to be a man of original ideas, with plenty of courage and energy to put them into operation.

The ability and remarkable activity that he evinced in this elevated position gained for William Merchant Richardson a reputation which is to-day one of the cherished possessions of the people of New Hampshire. It has lately been said of him by a writer well qualified to express an opinion that, with the exception of Judge Jeremiah Smith, perhaps no occupant of the judicial bench has done so much as he to shape the jurisprudence of that state.*

Chief Justice Richardson is to be remembered as a man of greater attainments than those of a mere lawyer. In various directions he may be styled a man of learning. He maintained through

---

* *Bench and Bar of New Hampshire, by Charles Henry Bell,* Boston, 1892, p. 72.

life a familiarity with the classics; and in a community where such accomplishments were by no
means frequent, he had become admirably well
versed in French, Italian and Spanish. Of botany
he knew much ; and he was something too of a
musician. Indeed, there were exhibited in Chief
Justice Richardson unusual intellectual powers
coupled with a deep-settled determination to be
useful by mastering thoroughly the subject in
hand, qualities destined to shine forth at a later
day in the person of his nephew, the late chief
justice of the Court of Claims.

Of General Samuel M. Richardson, the second
son, it may be briefly noted that he lived in Pelham,
where he achieved prominence as an active and
public-spirited citizen. For twelve years he was
sent as representative to the general court; he
became a state senator, and served in the war of
1812 as a major in the army. He likewise
enjoyed the rank of brigadier-general of the
militia. General Richardson died at Pelham, 11
March, 1858, leaving a handsome estate, a portion
of which he gave to charity. Of this will his
nephews, Daniel S. Richardson and William A.
Richardson, then both of Lowell, were executors
and trustees.

The third son, Daniel, father of the subject of
this sketch, if less conspicuous than his brothers,
was a man of like strength of character and of

much native ability. He studied law at Groton, in the office of Samuel Dana, at the time his brother, William Merchant Richardson, was Mr. Dana's law partner.

Upon admission to the bar young Richardson selected as the scene of his future professional triumphs the retired town of Tyngsborough, eight miles from Lowell, and twenty-five from Boston. The choice was certainly a modest one, for Tyngsborough though an attractive place of residence was not populous, nor had it showed signs of ever becoming such. It was almost exclusively an agricultural community. There were a saw and grist mill, and a small water-power shop, but they did not much disturb the quiet of the village. A stage from Amherst, New Hampshire, to Boston, passed through the town, and the Middlesex canal company had a wharf here—and these were the chief activities.

But young Richardson doubtless knew his limitations. He was at any rate resolute and fond of work. He exhibited traits of business that soon attracted the notice of the neighborhood, and before long clients had found their way to the country law office.* Indeed, if we may credit

---

* " His law office was situated in the store of the village merchant, that kind that kept cod-fish, silk, N. E. rum, and thread all on one shelf. The post-office was in the store. There were two other lawyers in town at that time, Charles Butterfield, (Harvard, 1820) brother of his first wife; and John Farwell, though neither of them practiced very much." *MS. letter of J. Franklin Bancroft*, 21 August, 1898.

the statement of a former sheriff of Middlesex (and nobody watches young lawyers more sharply than the sheriff), Daniel Richardson at the opening of the term of court used to enter more suits than any other lawyer in the county.

Mr. Richardson was one of that class of practitioners who can readily turn a hand to the performance of some useful or profitable duty not altogether within the strict line of the profession. He was made postmaster of the town; and he must have distributed the mail to general satisfaction since he held the appointment for the long period of thirty-five years. Of course, such a man found his way into the general court; and he went there as a whig representative of the town. He was elected state senator for two or three terms, and he occupied from time to time town offices of trust and responsibility.*

His was a life that knew no idle moments. At the age of fifty-nine years Daniel Richardson died at Tyngsborough, 12 February, 1842, respected and lamented by all who knew him. The first wife of Daniel Richardson was Betsey Butterfield, daughter of Asa and Abiah (Coburn) Butterfield of Tyngsborough, to whom he was married 10 May, 1810. She died young without issue. In April,

* "He owned several houses in the middle of the town, and was what was called in those days ' well to do.' "—*Ibid.*

1816, he was married to Mary,* second daughter of William and Mary (Roby) Adams of Chelmsford. Of this marriage there were two children, both born at Tyngsborough, Daniel Samuel, born 1 December, 1816, and William Adams, the subject of this sketch, born 2 November, 1821.

Says Mr. Bancroft:

When Daniel Richardson came to Tyngsborough he rented one-half of a house near the centre on the Dunstable road. This house was large, square and substantial, with "brick ends." It stood a little back from the road on a slight eminence commanding a fine view of a handsome sheet of water, with the wooded hills of the Tyng farm bounding the horizon to the south; nearer hills shut off the view and cold winds on the west, north and east. It was in this house that the Judge took his first gasp of New England weather in 1821.

---

* Mary (Adams) Richardson, the mother of the chief justice of the Court of Claims, was herself descended from Ezekiel, the first settler. Her father, William Adams, was a son of William and Elizabeth (Richardson) Adams of Chelmsford, Elizabeth Richardson being descended from John, Josiah and Ezekiel. Mary (Adams) Richardson's mother was Mary Roby, daughter of William and Hannah (Lund) Roby of Dunstable, now Nashua, New Hampshire. William Roby was a second lieutenant in a New Hampshire regiment at Bunker Hill, and afterwards first lieutenant in Col. Bedell's (N. H.) regiment, was taken prisoner in Canada and died in the service. William Adams, the maternal grandfather of the chief justice, was descended from Henry Adams, who came from Braintree in Essex, it is thought in 1634, and settled in that part of Braintree which is now Quincy, Massachusetts, the line being Henry, Samuel, Joseph, Benjamin, William. He was born at Chelmsford 30 April, 1762, and died there 25 December, 1843. When a lad of fifteen he enlisted as a revolutionary soldier, and served for six months. Then he enlisted again and served for eight months. In a family record, written by him in mature life, he says:

"While I was in service at West Point, I witnessed the execution of Major Andre, which made so lasting an impression on my mind that it is with tender and melancholy feelings that I look back upon that time."

He was a revolutionary pensioner.

Later in life " the Squire " moved into the village and occupied a house built by Mr. Adams, his father-in-law, who also owned the store, and perhaps kept it.*

When William was between three and four years of age, 1 August, 1825, his mother died. In November of the year following, his father was married to Hannah Adams, sister of the late wife, being the fourth daughter of the same parents. The only child of this marriage was George Francis Richardson, born 6 December, 1829 (Harvard, 1850), a prominent and able lawyer of Lowell, and a former mayor of that city.

Fortunately the child was not suffered to feel the absence of a mother's devotion, for a sister of his mother, as we see, had come into the household to bestow upon him care and nurture. Of William's boyhood few incidents have been preserved; and we are left to conclude that it resembled that of most New England lads brought up under discipline strict, yet kindly, in families of worth and refinement.†

---

* MS. letter of J. Franklin Bancroft, ante.

† Since this was written Mr. J. Franklin Bancroft, of Tyngsborough, has kindly favored the writer with a few particulars that afford us a glimpse of what sort of a youngster William Richardson must have been. The subtle flavor of Mr. Bancroft's style ought not to be spoiled by any attempt at editing :

"You ask me what kind of a boy the Judge was. I put the question in the same words to Mr. J. T. Lund, a very close friend of the Judge's in their school days. The answer was forcible, if not elegant—'A d—— good one.'

" Everybody says he was a real New England live Yankee boy. Thor-

Though not an expert at out-of-door sports, he was fond of skating, as what boy is not who has ever tasted the joys of a New England winter. One of his favorite occupations was to stuff birds. He must have been somewhat of a self-reliant youth. It is known at least that he early showed a disposition to be careful of the pennies that were given him, or that came in the way of earnings. A more trivial fact related of him is to the effect that when in common with other boys and girls he attended singing school, and took part in the exercises, the master would point at young Richardson and remark: "There is discord—right there."

---

oughly reliable, good disposition, good-hearted, always ready to help those in trouble, full of life and the devil, but nothing vicious in his make-up, he was open, frank and always ready to lead or follow, as the crowd desired. With this character it can be easily seen that he investigated the ins and outs of the land and water around his home.

"He was exceedingly popular in school among his classmates, and was liked by everybody, great and small. . . .

"That even as a boy he would not be coerced is shown by a little incident related to me by Mr. W. B. Cummings, better known as 'Uncle Brooks,' that happened when the Judge was ten or twelve years old. Even in those days the boys played ball, and the principal game was always played on Fast day, in the 'old field.'

"At this time preparations had been concluded at a singing school one evening, when a great lout of a 'bully,' who worked in a shop out of the center of the town, declared his intention of taking a hand in the game. The boys not liking him objected, and William told him squarely that they wouldn't have him. This brought out the 'bully,' and he catching William by the throat, threw him across a settee, and attempted to choke him into acquiescence, but no amount of choking could change his answer, and *No* was all he could get. Uncle Brooks thought it his duty to interfere at this point, and he says, 'I took the bully by the top end and fired him down stairs, telling him if he showed his face on the ball-field I would drown him.'"—*Ibid.*

At a tender age he was put at a primary school. Before he was eleven years old his father sent him away from home to study at Pinkerton Academy, where his brother Daniel had been educated, in the attractive town of Derry, in New Hampshire, not far from the Massachusetts line. The distance from Tyngsborough was some thirty miles or so, which meant a long way off, at a period when travel had to be accomplished by stage or by vehicle. The school, composed of about eighty boys, under the charge of Abel F. Hildreth (Harvard, 1818), an instructor of more than ordinary talent, appears to have been in a flourishing condition. Dr. Hildreth had earned for the academy a high reputation during his administration from 1819 to 1846.*

A more wholesome place could hardly have been selected than Derry—a town built up by sturdy and independent families of Scotch-Irish descent, whose children to this day are noted for thrift and prosperity.

The name of William Adams Richardson first

---

* " He was a singularly successful teacher, and while he lived and labored here he made his institution second to none other in New England."
—*Daniel S. Richardson*, 12 September, 1861,—Semi-Centennial Anniversary of Pinkerton Academy (Concord, 1866), p. 55.

Judge Richardson writing a letter of regret from Boston, 31 August, 1866, shows his practical turn of mind by saying : " I wish the trustees would follow the example of other academies and print a catalogue of all the graduates of the institution, with their present residences, etc. Such catalogues are very interesting and are the best advertisements which can be printed and circulated." (*Ibid.*, p. 106.)

appears upon the list of the academy students for the school year 1833–1834, which began in August; and it is also found recorded for the two following years.   Says John C. Chase, of Derry:

Among those who were at the academy at the same time with Richardson who have been heard from in after life I find the names of John M. Pinkerton, who at his death, some fifteen years ago, gave his estate, amounting to about $150,000, to the institution that had been founded and endowed by his father and uncle; Nathaniel G. White, for many years president of the Boston & Maine Railroad; Aaron F. Stevens, of Nashua, a member of Congress; Joseph B. Walker, of Concord; Edwin F. French, brother of Henry F. French, late of Washington; Judge Samuel F. Humphrey, of Bangor, Maine. There are only two pupils of his time now resident in town, and they have no recollection of him. *

In the summer of 1833, a tremendous stir was created throughout New England by the visit of Andrew Jackson, then President of the United States.   The chief magistrate had not the facilities for going about the country that are now so common, and Jackson was cordially hated by most of his political opponents, whose sole idea of him had been derived from their party newspapers. At all events, it was for many people a great privilege to get a sight of "Old Hickory."   Upon his reaching Cambridge, Harvard College, it will be recalled, conferred upon him the degree of doctor of laws, the only honorary degree given that year.   It so happened that William Richardson,

* MS. letter, 21 July, 1897.

then a boy of eleven years, was at home from school, probably upon a vacation, at the time of the coming of the President. The following incident is related of General Jackson's journey:

The course of the presidential party toward Nashua was that generally travelled, on the south side of the Merrimack river. While passing through Tyngsborough a boy came out upon an eminence which commanded a fair view of the President and his companions. He had in his hand a fowling-piece, having been out hunting that morning without a thought, however, of the possibility of coming upon the lion which he so suddenly confronted. When the President's barouche came opposite, the lad snatched off his cap, swung it in the air, and gave three as vigorous " hurrahs " as his small voice would permit, at the same time discharging his gun.

Observing the act of the boy, the President removed his hat and bowed with as much formality as he would have done had there been a regiment before him. The boy who was favored with this consideration was the Honorable William A. Richardson, a native of the town, late Secretary of the Treasury of the United States.*

After William Richardson had attained to man's estate few persons of discernment could have talked with him without instantly perceiving that from boyhood he must have acquired and exercised the habits of a student. The presence of this trait, however, is not to be left to inference. Among sundry papers labelled and laid away by the late chief justice for preservation, is one yellow with age, and bearing an

* From a paper read before the Old Residents' Historical Society of Lowell, in 1875, by Mr. Z. E. Stone, entitled " The Visit of President Jackson to Lowell in June, 1833." The paper is printed in the published " Contributions " of that society, Vol. II, p. 152.

inscription in his handwriting, "This is the first letter I ever received. W. A. R." Any young man might well have prized it. The sheet appears to have been originally sealed with a wafer. It is addressed, "Master Wm. A. Richardson, Derry, N. H., Pr. politeness of your father." The letter reads thus :

TYNGSBORO, *June 4th, 1834.*

Mr. WILLIAM A. RICHARDSON,

My respected young friend,

I am happy for the present opportunity to write to one with whom I have had so many hours of pleasure and delight. Your good nature, high spirit, lively turn, all serve to raise you above those of your mates in my estimation. Always ready to oblige you can not but demand the obligation and esteem of others. Always happy and cheerful you shed much happiness and good feeling around you.

I am happy to learn that you continue to maintain abroad the same cheerfulness as at home. Prompt to obey your teacher, and never caught in mischievous or low bred company.

I am happy to learn likewise that you are determined to embrace the advice of your parents and make the best of your new superior advantages. In so doing you will make yourself wise and honourable in after life not only on your own account but by gratifying the wishes and expectations of your parents.

I remain sir with much esteem, very respectfully yours,

SAML. ELLIOT.*

In haste

Please write when you have an opportunity.

---

* "Popularly known as 'Deacon Elliot,' though he had no connection with the church. He was the village store-keeper, and kept the store in which was the post-office. He was a member of the school committee, well educated himself, a friend of education, always encouraging the pupils to 'hitch their wagon to a star.' He removed from here to Elmira, N. Y., and died shortly after." *MS. letter of J. Franklin Bancroft,* 21 **August,** 1898.

Master Richardson was then in his thirteenth year. How fragrant even to this hour the act of writing and sending that letter. The boy never forgot the day that it had been put into his hand. "This is the first letter I ever received." Kind and considerate friend, your text, after the fashion of the day, may be a little stilted, but your honest and well-timed praise found its way to a boy's heart. Who can say that it did not mightily help him to become "wise and honourable in after life." Truly, a word spoken in due season, how good is it.

Before the summer of 1837 had closed, the schoolboy now advanced to his sixteenth year, was transferred to new quarters, in order to complete the course of study required for admission to Harvard College. The academy at Groton, Massachusetts, besides that the town was nearer home, held out peculiar advantages, both of an educational and of a social character; and accordingly young Richardson was entered there as a student. Groton is a delightful town; and we know, from his later utterances, that it must have been to him a scene of almost unalloyed enjoyment. At that date about a hundred scholars, nearly equally divided between boys and girls, attended the academy. Mr. Horace Herrick, a recent graduate from Dartmouth College, was the preceptor, assisted by Miss Clarissa Butler.

The institution known as "The Groton Academy," a name borne from its foundation, maintained a deservedly high repute throughout that part of the country. After Richardson had left it, the name was changed, in 1846, to "The Lawrence Academy," in recognition of the munificence of the Lawrences, of Boston, natives of Groton, who in their gifts to this institution of learning signalized, as they had done in numerous other instances, the noble uses to which wealth can be applied.

When young Richardson began his studies at Groton, the railroad, it is to be remembered, had not yet come in to change the relative importance of New England towns. Seated upon the direct line of travel, the main street of the village presented a busy scene of passing wagons and stage coaches, while the taverns were centres of no little activity and bustle. Indeed the life and stir of a Groton tavern must have wrought a deep impression upon the student mind, to judge from what may be found in a book of reminiscences of the academy, published in 1893, at the date of its hundredth anniversary.

Says Judge Richardson :

The most prominent and conspicuous in the town were the stage drivers and tavern keepers ; I remember well Mr. Joseph Hoar, who kept one of the village inns, The Central House, and who was always with an unlighted stump of a cigar in his mouth. I used to wonder who smoked all the

cigars from which he had so many stumps, for he was never
seen with a lighted cigar, and I think he never smoked nor
drank.

Then there was Thomas O. Staples, proprietor of the line
of stages from Boston to Keene, with its famous Concord
coaches, a man of splendid physique and a distinguished
driver. His wife, too, could handle the reins nearly as well
as her husband and occasionally she drove the coach and six
from Boston to Groton, to the admiration and astonishment
of everybody who saw or knew her.

Judge Richardson was one of the active promoters of a celebration by the alumni at Groton
in 1854. He was the leading spirit also in carrying forward to a successful result a similar
celebration of the two anniversaries, that of 1883
and that of 1893. His heart ever warmed to the
scenes of his boyhood, nor could any one have
enjoyed more keenly the pleasure of meeting old
classmates; while they in like manner when they
have occasion to write or speak of him do so in
very affectionate terms.

One of the pleasing incidents of his life at
Groton is described by him as the festival of the
crowning of the king and queen of May on the
first day of May, 1839. He writes of it 1 May,
1893, exactly fifty-four years later: "After a
march up the street to the fields where the wild
flowers could be gathered, the boys and girls
returned. Then a girl placed upon the head of a
boy a wreath of flowers, while young Richardson
placed on the head of a girl a similar wreath."

The Judge mentions the pleasing fact that after fifty-four years had passed all four were then living and in good health. It may be added here that he was in the habit in later years of sending his family to Groton for the summer, and of going there himself for such vacations as he could be persuaded to take.

Richardson was admitted to the freshman class of Harvard College in the summer of 1839, and was graduated in 1843. Of the sixty-nine who took degrees, thirty were living at the fiftieth anniversary of their graduation. Among the more prominent members of the class there may be mentioned Charles A. Dana, of the *New York Sun;* Octavius B. Frothingham, Unitarian minister and writer; Arthur B. Fuller, chaplain of the sixteenth Massachusetts regiment, who died at Fredericksburg, Virginia, in 1862; Thomas Hill (a life-long friend of the subject of this sketch) afterward (1861–8) president of Harvard College; John W. Kingman, territorial governor of Wyoming; John Lowell, United States circuit judge; Charles C. Perkins, widely known as a writer upon art; Horace Binney Sargent, of Boston; E. Carleton Sprague, a leader of the Buffalo Bar; Eben F. Stone, of Newburyport, a lawyer, active at the bar of Essex and in the state legislature, later a member of Congress; and Alexander W. Thayer, musical author and critic.

Richardson's chum throughout the four years' course was William Henry Adams, of North Chelmsford, who was with him at Groton academy. He died in 1845.

It does not appear that Richardson made any special mark in college.* He was quiet in his ways, and studious, but disinclined to struggle for honors, either of the college or of the class. Some time after graduation his classmates elected him class secretary, a post of honor which he held for many years and until his death. It is hardly necessary to add that he performed the duties of the office, which called for no inconsiderable labor on his part, with a scrupulous care and promptitude. Upon the occasion of the fiftieth anniversary (1893) it was Chief Justice Richardson, their secretary, whom the class had selected to speak for them at the commencement dinner.

His successor as class secretary writes :

I saw little of him in our college life. . . . In 1883, he prepared and distributed a "Memorabilia" pamphlet of the class for the meeting that year, and issued a similar report of the class meeting in 1893.

The lines of our lives have not brought us in contact since graduating, except casually. He was a painstaking and persistent laborer where interested. He certainly was ambitious to leave a good record.†

---

*One of his classmates, since (1898) deceased, John A Loring, a lawyer of Boston, informed the writer that Richardson in his freshman year began to work upon the revised statutes of Massachusetts, and that probably no other living person than Mr. L. knew of the fact.

† MS. letter, 14 August, 1897, of Thomas B. Hall, secretary of the Class of '43.

Another classmate, who has since died, said of him :

I should be pleased to give you any facts in regard to my classmate Richardson which might be interesting to his friends, but he was a retiring man and had but few intimates, and I do not know that I was among the number, though our relations were perfectly friendly. He went to Cambridge to study, and he studied conscientiously; was what in those days was called a " dig"; always prepared with his task, rather by dint of hard work than by facility of acquisition. I doubt if Sargent, who graduated our first scholar, ever devoted the time to study that Richardson did.

I do not ever remember seeing him engaged in any game, either athletic or intellectual. He wrote a small, crabbed, school-boy hand.

" Richardson," said Professor Johnson, one day, looking over one of his themes in the presence of the class, " Richardson, I don't think your handwriting is just the thing for elegant literature." A trifling incident that survives nearly fifty-five years, while so many things that are worth remembering, have escaped and are forgotten.*

This well-meant criticism from the professor may not have been without its effect, for in later years his handwriting could not be said to have given cause for complaint. Indeed it had become a good, legible hand, plain but strong, well suited to the purposes of one who worked in a study and wrote much for the printer.

Although Mr. Richardson may not have been conspicuous among his classmates, or taken high rank as a scholar, it is evident that he had imbibed at Cambridge a deep and abiding affection

* MS. letter of John J. Russell, Plymouth, Massachusetts, 20 July, 1897.

for Harvard College. His life as an undergraduate was we may be sure a pleasant one, seeing as we do so many tokens that his college associations were in after life dear to him. He was loyal to the best traditions of Harvard. For twelve years (1863–1875) he served as a member of the board of overseers, elected for the first term of six years by the legislature, and for the second term by the alumni.

At this post his labors were constant, and at all times well directed. Upon removal to Washington, he remitted nothing of his vigilance in watching every change proposed at Harvard, of which it is to be said that more than one perhaps owed its first impulse to some suggestion from him. By means of active correspondence he sought to help forward plans for broadening and strengthening the institution in various directions. Few friends of the university whether of its official family, or outside, had bestowed more elaborate thought upon the legal relations of the college, its charter and its property rights, as well as upon various questions which arose from time to time in respect to the need of organic changes in the administration of its affairs.

Subjects of historic interest, pertaining to the college, or her graduates, also occupied largely Mr. Richardson's attention. He prepared and published a list of the alumni who had held high

public position, state or federal,—data of perceptible value, as attested by similar lists from
other universities, the work of compilers who
followed his footsteps. He was one of the earliest
promoters of the plan of taking the election of
overseers out of the control of the legislature,
and entrusting it to the hands of the alumni.
Nor did matters of minor concern escape his eye,
wherever an actual improvement could reasonably be counted upon. He appears to have been
the first graduate to advocate earnestly the printing of the Quinquennial in English, and he lived
to see the change effected.

Immediately upon being graduated, Richardson began a course of reading at the law office
of his brother Daniel, at Lowell. For a while
also he studied in the offices, at Boston, of Fuller
and Andrew, the junior partner being John A.
Andrew, afterwards the famous war governor of
Massachusetts. After 4 March, 1845, he entered
the Harvard law school, whose professors were
Joseph Story (who died in September following),
and Simon Greenleaf. Here he remained for
eighteen months, taking the degree of bachelor of
laws at the end of that period, according to the
easy requirements then in force. Upon motion
of Mr. Andrew, who was six years his senior in
the profession, Mr. Richardson was admitted to
the Suffolk bar 8 July, 1846. On the next day,

at Lowell, his partnership with his brother, Daniel S. Richardson (Harvard, 1836), was announced, and he was to be found at his desk, ready to serve a client. The alliance was in the nature of a fortunate opening for the younger member of the firm, since his brother, a lawyer of fine abilities and a man of lovable character, had not only established himself in a lucrative and growing practice, but had come to be extremely popular with the bar.

Well educated, eager for work, modest, and with slight taste for public speaking,—certainly with no inclination for facing a jury,—one may conceive what kind of practice fell to the junior member of the firm. What with making collections, drawing leases and deeds, looking up titles, attending to the probate of wills and the administration of estates, young Richardson, painstaking and methodical to the utmost, had no reason to complain of his prospects.

After three years of practice, the future chief justice, it appears, felt equal to supporting a wife. He was married 29 October, 1849, to Anna Maria Marston, daughter of Jonathan and Sarah (Holt) Marston, of Machiasport, Maine.* The union

---

*Their only child, Isabella Anna, was born in Lowell on 21st December, 1850; died at Washington, D. C., 4 April, 1898. She was married 23 November, 1876, to Alexander F. Magruder, passed assistant surgeon United States navy, son of the late Dr. Magruder, of Georgetown, D. C., and a descendant, on his mother's side, of the Fitzhugh family, of Virginia. They had three children : William Richardson Magruder, born in

proved to be most happy in every respect. Mrs.
Richardson possessed qualities of both person
and mind that fitted her to be, in the best sense
of the word, a helpmate. Whether in their quiet
home life at Lowell, or at a later period when
called upon to meet social obligations at Washington, as the wife of a member of the cabinet, or of the
chief justice of the Court of Claims, she was always
equal to her duties. Handsome and accomplished, Mrs. Richardson's cordial manner of wel-
coming the visitor, together with her animated
and genuine interest in the welfare of those
around her, won for her a large circle of friends,
and redounded greatly to the advantage of her
husband.

The conduct of a man thus occupied with his
own affairs is watched, and, if he is seen to be
diligent and faithful, he is wanted before long for
this or that minor public position. In 1849, Mr.
Richardson was elected to the common council of
the city of Lowell. Again elected in 1853 and
1854, he was made president of the board. The
circumstance is interesting, and perhaps is without
a parallel in our municipal history, that three

Washington, D. C., 20 December, 1878; died in Groton, Massachusetts,
1883; Alexander Richardson Magruder, born in Nice, France, while his
father was stationed there on duty, 17 January, 1883; Isabella Richardson
Magruder, born in Washington, D. C., 20 April, 1886.

Dr. Magruder was retired as full surgeon. He went upon the active
list, however, at the breaking out of the Spanish war, and served at the
marine headquarters, Washington.

brothers [Daniel S., William A., and George F.] should each in turn have held this honorable position. Meanwhile, he had been made (1846–1850) judge advocate of a division of the militia with the rank of major; while Governor Briggs later appointed him an aide-de-camp with the rank of lieutenant colonel, a gold-laced position which brings a young man into wider notice. The trustees of the Lowell Five Cent Savings Bank elected him one of their number; and he served for several years on the finance committee of that institution.

He had been early chosen a director of the Appleton Bank. Subsequently, he resigned that position in order to accept the presidency of the Wamesit Bank, afterwards the Wamesit National Bank, which office he held until 1867, when he returned to the Appleton, that had meanwhile become the Appleton National Bank. With this institution he continued as director until his appointment as Secretary of the Treasury, when he resigned the office and sold out his stock. His experience in the management of these banks, and of the savings bank previously named, developed a sagacity and acuteness that served him in good stead when called upon subsequently to deal with the vast business of the treasury of the United States.

At a somewhat later period he was chosen

president of the Middlesex Mechanic's Association, an honor in itself the more to be valued because it gave him opportunity to assist in the reorganization of that important body. This office he filled for two years.

In May, 1855, Mr. Richardson it seems made his first venture as an author, or let us rather say, compiler. With the sanction, and perhaps at the instance of the bank commissioners of the state, he prepared and published a handy volume upon the banking laws of Massachusetts, being a compilation of the statutes relating to banks and savings institutions, with notes of decisions, etc. The modest little book, which doubtless served a useful purpose in its day and is now chiefly noteworthy as a model of arrangement and indexing, was published at Lowell and Boston.

Employments such as these had no effect to divert him from a punctual and devoted attention to the wants of his clients. Whatever else Judge Richardson may have been, he always remained the lawyer, with a liking for the application of legal principles to the daily concerns of life. The prospect of litigation did not attract him ; where he found pleasure was in facilitating the prompt and safe transaction of the every-day business affairs of those who sought his professional aid. Here he was getting an admirable training when a summons to engage in work of larger scope came to him most unexpectedly, though it found him, we may believe, prepared fairly well for the task.

The tendency of state legislatures to make changes at every session in the statutes, whether by way of repeal or amendment, or by bringing forward entirely new provisions of law, has become proverbial; and Massachusetts, it must be confessed, at no period of her political history furnishes an exception to the rule. By this time the statute law of the commonwealth had grown into an unwieldy mass, so that particular provisions were difficult of ascertainment, and when found, were fruitful of perplexities. The only remedy was revision. Already the governor had appointed commissioners to determine upon a plan in accordance with which the revision might best be accomplished. Upon a report from them the legislature, 16 February, 1855, passed a resolution empowering the governor to appoint three commissioners to consolidate and rearrange the statutes, with authority to—

Omit redundant enactments and those which may have ceased to have effect or influence on existing rights; to reject superfluous words, and to condense into as concise and comprehensive a form, as is consistent with a full and clear expression of the legislature, all circuitous, tautological and ambiguous phraseology; to suggest any mistakes, omissions, inconsistencies and imperfections which may appear in the laws to be consolidated and arranged, and the manner in which they may be corrected, supplied and amended.

These terms indicate to what lengths the responsibility extended and how broad a discretion was to be reposed in the commission. Governor Gardner, on the 9th of March following, named for the office Joel Parker, of Cambridge, Royal professor of law at Harvard and formerly chief justice of New Hampshire; William A. Richardson, of Lowell; and Andrew A. Richmond, of Adams.*

The appointees accepted the office and entered at once upon the work, although Mr. Richmond's health prevented his taking an active part therein. A disproportionate share consequently fell upon Mr. Richardson. But the junior commissioner felt no discouragement at what confronted him; on the contrary the work laid out was exactly to his taste; and he bent himself with unflagging energy to go through the body of the statutes so

---

* As illustrating the truth that chance sometimes has much to do with a young man's opportunity for advancement, the following remarks once made by the chief justice as to how he happened to be appointed to this important office, at the age of thirty-four, may not inappropriately find room here: "I do not think that the governor (Henry J. Gardner) had ever heard of me, until some one, a senator, suggested my name as a candidate. I came very near not getting that appointment. When the senator first mentioned my name the governor said he had just settled upon the list of names, and it was too late to make a change in it. There were three commissioners. A few days afterwards the governor sent for the senator, and asked more about me, saying that after all he might make a change in the list; and he did so, and I was named as one. When the appointments came out afterward, I learned in course of time that between the first and second interview with the senator, the governor had some trouble with one of the three he had selected, a man from Newton, a warm personal friend up to that time, and on that account had struck his name off the list and substituted mine."

as to have a report ready by the autumn of 1858. Of course, such an undertaking was to the last degree laborious. Indeed, considering how much there was for a single man to do, it must always remain a marvel that the volume, which ultimately grew out of the work of the commission, proved so admirable in plan, and so faultless in execution. The volume referred to is the General Statutes of the Commonwealth of Massachusetts of 1860, embodied in an act passed 28 December, 1859.

The duty of editing and superintending the printing of the statutes, forming as they do a book of upwards of eleven hundred pages, was entrusted to William A. Richardson and George P. Sanger. Circumstances obliged them to send the sheets to the printer under a pressure of some haste, but the completed volume shows no sign of it. They prefixed the constitution of the United States and that of Massachusetts, furnished chapter headings in detail, and supplied to the text, both of the constitutions and of the statutes, copious notes, citations and cross-references. To this they added a glossary and an index, the latter having the merit of accuracy and fulness.

While praise is unquestionably due to Judge Sanger for his share of the undertaking, no one who knows the requirements of such a task, and who besides has seen what Judge Richardson

at a later period accomplished in his revision
of the statutes of the United States, will be at
a loss to determine what proportion of the design is to be credited to him. Unlike previous
revisions, many of which went little further than
to rearrange the several enactments, the report
made by Messrs. Parker and Richardson amounted
to a re-writing of nearly the whole body of the
statute law.* In several instances they changed
the language of the statutes, especially under the
head of criminal law. Notwithstanding some
opposition in the legislature, every one of these
changes was approved, and most of them afterwards justified themselves as being of practical
value.

It was a subject of pride with Chief Justice
Richardson that in his younger days the honor
should have been his of taking part in this
severe and protracted labor of revision; and
that the volume in the preparation of which he
applied himself with so much ardor, had stood
the test of time and proved to be substantially, if
not literally, free from error.

---

* One day during the early sessions of the board, Judge Parker, the
chairman, handed to Mr. Richardson a chapter drawn up informally and
told him to take it up and see what he could do with it. This was said
at the State House in Boston. Mr. Richardson took the manuscript that
night to Lowell, twenty-five miles away, and sat up all night working
upon it. The next morning he brought it back to Boston compressed into
about three pages. It was adopted and printed as he had written it, and
ever since has formed a chapter in the statutes as revised.

Some one has well said of it : " The amount of labor, patient study and legal skill required in mastering so much complication, and bringing the mass into harmonious order, may be imagined by all; but its successful accomplishment can only be appreciated by an experienced legal mind."

Judge Richardson continued to edit and superintend the issue of an annual volume of the Massachusetts statutes for a period of twenty-two years. The stereotype plates of the General Statutes of 1860 were destroyed by the great fire at Boston in 1872. Pursuant to an act of the legislature he edited, in conjunction with Judge Sanger, a new edition in 1873, as well as a supplementary volume of legislative enactments since 1860. This last-named labor was accomplished, it should be stated, at a time when the editor-in-chief was at Washington, immersed in the business of the Treasury Department.

Later achievements in the line of statutory revision may conveniently be noted here. It is doubtful whether there can be named a lawyer in successful practice, or a judge upon the bench who has ever exhibited a willingness, nay, let it rather be termed a desire, comparable to that of Chief Justice Richardson, to undergo the drudgery of bringing into orderly and systematic arrangement the vast material of the statute law. To begin with, it is a species of unmitigated

toil that only a select few would think of undertaking. Without reckoning a conception of the
plan as a whole, the almost endless detail which
is of necessity involved, exacts of one an amount
of manual labor that would deter most men from
thinking of taking upon themselves this burden,
even with competent assistance.

An ability to carry along in the memory the
meaning, not to say the precise wording, of an
enactment, with a view of fitting to it a note or
reference, or the disconnected terms of some other
statute, is a gift rarely possessed. But Chief Justice
Richardson had this gift; and, what is more, he
had an unerring perception of where a line of
text belonged. He was endowed, too, with an
instinct, one is almost tempted to call it genius,
for indexing. Besides, he has more than once
displayed a rare judgment in the difficult art of
book-making. He knew exactly how to arrange
printed material in dress and collocation so as
to wear the most attractive look of which it is
capable; while the system of catch-lines and mar-
ginal annotations that he employed, and to a large
extent originated, is such that he who has frequent occasion to use the volume, almost conceives
a friendly feeling for the author.

Soon after the passage of the revised statutes of
the United States (1874) it became a daily habit
with Judge Richardson to watch the legislation of

Congress while in session, and to enter references thereto upon his note-book. This work he kept up for the rest of his life because he liked it. It is safe to say that probably no one in the United States at any day during this period had in hand such a thorough knowledge of the exact condition of the federal statute law as Judge Richardson. With the progress of time these annotations grew to be of large volume, and correspondingly valuable. The collection was unique. Nobody else apparently had thought to do the like. Congress, when made aware of its existence, took steps to provide for its official publication. Acts were passed directing that the statutes of the United States should be printed with the annotations of Judge Richardson, and under his direction, and that the work should be stereotyped.

Owing to his forethought and his persistent labor, day after day, the bar is now enabled to consult in a very convenient form, supplements of the revised statutes of the United States from 1874 to 1895. Moreover, this admirable plan of publication once adopted has now apparently become the settled policy of Congress. The work, it is true, meets the eye of but a limited number of people. The world at large knows and cares little about it; still, lawyers, judges, legislators and public officials turn to these volumes with more or less frequency; and, it may truthfully be added, always with satisfaction. It is difficult to see in what particular the plan, as devised by Chief Justice Richardson, can be improved upon. Although the work is destined in time to be supplanted, a new compilation must perforce follow the lines of the old. For this reason "Richardson's Supplements" are likely to remain a monument to the honor of him who conceived a well-nigh faultless plan of bringing to the public a knowledge of the provisions of the federal statutes.

In the spring of 1856 Judge Samuel Phillips Prescott Fay (Harvard, 1793) resigned the office of judge of probate for Middlesex county; an office which he had held since 1821, for a period of nearly thirty-five years. Governor Gardner appointed Mr. Richardson, 7 April, 1856, to fill the vacancy. The choice met the general consent and approval of the bar. The new incumbent, already favorably known to the governor by his labors upon the commission to revise the statutes, had demonstrated satisfactorily to the people of Lowell and the county in general that he was peculiarly well suited to the position. The change from office practice to a seat upon the bench was, we may believe, very acceptable to the incoming judge. He was glad to be thus honored in his own county, and he welcomed the multiplied and arduous duties that awaited him.

A judge of probate, it need hardly be explained, ought to know a good deal more than the rules of law governing the administration of estates. He not only sits to act upon petitions and decide controversies, but people resort to him daily, "the widow and the orphan," for advice and counsel. A selfish man, or one of stern demeanor, would not be tolerated there; an impulsive, tender-hearted judge, lacking in firmness, would be equally out of place. Happily Judge Richardson possessed just the qualities needed for a successful administration of the office.*

---

*Governor Frederick T. Greenhalge, who, before entering into public life had reached distinction as a lawyer at Lowell, said at a memorial meeting of the bar upon the occasion of the death of George M. Brooks: "Judge Brooks succeeded a most remarkable man, singularly adapted to the work of the probate court—Judge William A. Richardson—and yet no one ever fulfilled with more success, with more conscious exactness to law, fact, sympathy and efficacy of action, the work assigned him than Judge Brooks."

Says A. V. Lynde (November, 1897) a prominent practitioner and one of the oldest lawyers at the Middlesex bar: "Richardson was the best judge of probate they ever had in Massachusetts. His power of despatching business was tremendous. There was a case in which George P. Burnham (who had gained local notoriety during the 'Shanghai chicken' craze), was a party. The question was whether a sum of $10,000 should be allowed in a probate account. On one side was Butler, Rockwood Hoar, Brooks and other strong counsel. I had as an associate Theodore H. Sweetser. We had more than forty hearings before Judge Richardson, he not intimating in the least what his opinion would be. At the last hearing, upon the close of the argument, Richardson said, 'I shall not allow this claim,' adjourned court, and took his hat and left the court house."

Mr. Lynde spoke of talking one day with Judge Richardson about his method of disposing of cases rapidly. The judge said he preferred in probate hearings to give an immediate opinion. "Are you not sometimes wrong?" asked Mr. Lynde. "Oh, yes," replied the judge, "I suppose that sometimes I decide wrong, but in the majority of cases, I think my first impressions are right; and then it is best to get through them quickly, or cases would consume too much time in argument."

The judge was a critical observer of the means employed in the administration of judicial affairs. He studied practice closely. He believed in extending, where it could safely be done, the field into which his court should enter. He was not a man content to settle down into old-fashioned ways of doing business, when after careful inspection he had once satisfied himself that a method could be improved. Accordingly his busy ingenuity conceived a plan of enlarging the jurisdiction of the probate court; and he was largely instrumental in securing action by the legislature conferring upon that tribunal concurrent jurisdiction with that of the supreme court, in the construction of wills and the administration of estates. To his wisely directed influence it is due that the probate court in Massachusetts has acquired an exclusive original jurisdiction over many subjects that formerly it did not enjoy.

It was left also to Judge Richardson to propose to his fellow judges of probate a scheme of uniformity in the matter of practice. He had seen that each one of the fourteen counties had its own forms, which had been followed since the days of the Revolution. The blanks in use varied with each court, and there was an absence of uniformity in almost every particular. Each judge was naturally inclined to treat the settled forms of his own court as the best to be devised;

and the young Middlesex official who urged the benefits of regularity and uniformity had to encounter a weighty opposition. Many of the older practitioners likewise were conservative, and viewed any proposed modification with scant favor.

But the earnestness and persistency of the advocate for reform prevailed; the judges met, and upon his motion named a committee to revise the probate blanks and make them uniform throughout the state. They selected Richardson, of course, together with Judges John Wells and Samuel F. Lyman, both of them new to the bench, though the latter had been a register of probate for many years. Having started the project, Judge Richardson, as generally happens in such cases, was allowed by his associates to go ahead and do all the work,—which he did, and what is more, did it gratuitously. We may gather from the following memorandum of the judge himself what must have been the nature of the undertaking,—a task much more onerous, it will be observed, than perhaps would at first have been suspected :

Two judges, both older than myself, were put on the committee and I, who alone had experience in the probate court, was added. My associates were both from the western part of the state, and we were all three far separate, so that we could not meet for consultation.

I made an arrangement with the state printer in Boston to print the blanks, in expectation that the counties would take their respective shares, for we had no money at our disposal for the expenses. Of course, the whole labor fell upon me, who alone had an office in Boston, and was familiar with the practice of the probate courts, and had started the scheme myself. I had already formed my opinions as to the blanks generally. Up to that time each of the fourteen counties had its own system and its own blanks, and they had been diverging from each other for two hundred years or so. Of course, there was very little similarity,—none except such as the statutes required or suggested.

The very first set of blanks that I had printed and sent to each of the judges, raised opposition from two counties ; all the others were quite satisfied. One of my associates resigned from the committee, saying that he could not agree to such radical changes of forms which were older than the constitution of the state. The other associate made no objection, and I rarely saw him. Once in a great while, when in Boston from one of the extreme western counties, he came into my office, but he had no opportunity to do anything, and being a new man without experience in court, he had no suggestions to make.

I worked over these blanks for more than a year. When completed I took them to Chief Justice Bigelow of the supreme court, who was a friend of mine, for adoption by that court, in accordance with a provision of the statutes which had been in force for a quarter of a century without any action taken. Bigelow adopted, or rather approved them at once, and for the court ordered them [11 April, 1861] to be adopted in all the counties. One county, Essex, still manifested hostility and came into the plan with great reluctance. Bigelow, who was constantly inquiring, whenever we met, as to how I was getting on, told me that if the judge in Essex did not adopt the forms, he would issue a mandamus to show cause, and would compel him to adopt them. But I did not want to press matters, and they finally got into use even there.

Some years afterwards (nearly twenty years), the supreme court held that the forms as thus adopted were part of the law of the state, and could not be changed but by that court, as they were so ordered to be adopted. (*Baxter* v. *Blood*, 128 Mass. 543.)

The principal advantages gained were and are, absolute uniformity of forms in the whole fourteen counties. In the blanks themselves some matters may be mentioned as among the most important changes: Stating the exact date of the death of the decedents. Before, no date was given. Naming all the heirs and next of kin, with the place of residence, and the husbands of married women. In these particulars the probate records of Massachusetts will in time prove a mine for exploration by the genealogists.

The judge had occupied the office scarcely two years when the legislature effected a radical change in the system of the probate courts by consolidating them with the courts of insolvency, and creating a court of probate and insolvency, of which Judge Richardson was made a judge for Middlesex. The real object in view was to bring about, by act of the legislature, the removal of Edward Greely Loring (Harvard, 1831), judge of probate for Suffolk county, a man of ability and of the highest integrity. As a matter of fact Judge Loring was removed from office by Governor Banks, 19 March, 1858, upon a supersedeas, in compliance with the address of the legislature.*

---

* Loring was, however, not long deprived of judicial honors. A vacancy having recently occurred on the bench of the Court of Claims at Washington, through the death of Chief Justice Gilchrist, of New Hampshire, the President named Loring to be a judge of that court, and he was confirmed 6 May, 1858. In this capacity he served the country honorably and well. He relinquished his seat, after having passed the age limit, in 1877. Alike on the bench or in retirement, the judge was a man of charming personality, a raconteur of the very highest order. He, with his wife and daughters, each brilliant and witty, rendered the Loring home, on K street, a centre of social delight, unsurpassed elsewhere at the Capital.

Judge Loring held the office likewise of commissioner of the circuit court of the United
States, and in his capacity as such had rendered
a decision which had the effect to return Anthony
Burns to his owner under the fugitive slave law,
a decision the circumstances of which created
intense excitement in Massachusetts, and have
been to this day held in remembrance as forming
one of the dramatic preludes to the war for the
Union. The action of the commissioner, though
in obedience to the plain dictates of the law, and
governed by the purest motives on his part, was
bitterly resented by the people.

Because he had discharged his duty Judge Loring suffered an odium as profound as it was unjust.
The newspapers poured upon him a stream of violent denunciation. Wendell Phillips, the orator
without a peer, stirred the people almost as never
before, with words of scornful acrimony and fiery
wrath. Every abolitionist had wrought himself,
and a good many of his neighbors, up to the
highest pitch of resentful indignation. Some
safety-valve had to be supplied for so tremendous a pressure of explosive material; and from
all over the state came a stern demand for the
removal of the offending judge.

The legislature passed an address to the governor, asking that Judge Loring be removed, in
accordance with the constitution of Massachu-

setts, which provides that any judge may be removed by the governor upon the address of both houses of the legislature. Governor Henry J. Gardner, who it seems was a conservative man, refused to execute the will of the legislature, as he had a right to do. He believed that Loring had done nothing more than he was bound to do under the law; and that this act he had performed not in the capacity of a judge of probate, but as a United States commissioner, over whose conduct in office the state had no control whatever. The governor, therefore, declined to take action.

The members of the legislature, who had been elected in the autumn of 1857, came together in January, 1858, fresh from the excited people, and burning with vengeance against Loring, whose removal they were determined to accomplish. They meant to make an example of him. No matter what might stand in the way, they were bound to have his official head taken off.

But a respectable number of men in the legislature and outside entertained more conservative views; while sympathizing with the feeling against Loring, they were not willing to have him removed by address. Circumstances favored them at least in one respect. There were in each county a judge of probate and a judge of insolvency. Those favoring a moderate course conceived the idea of uniting the two offices, and having but one judge in each county, under the pretence, that while one judge could do all the business, the expense of two courts, or of two judges, would thus be reduced; and moreover, that by raising the salary of a single judge above the sum then paid to each of the two, the people would secure a better class of judges. The real object, of course, was to remove all the judges, among whom would be the obnoxious Loring, at whom alone the scheme was aimed.

This proposal, ingenious though it was, by no means appeased the members bent upon vengeance. They announced themselves disposed to agree to the new plan of abolishing and consolidating the courts, but they demanded that the address for Loring's removal should be first passed. The chairman of the committee upon the consolidation scheme, Eben F. Stone, of Newburyport (a classmate of Judge Richardson), sent out circulars to the judges asking their views. They all replied opposing the scheme, with the single exception of Richardson. Seeing that the result must come, and could by no possibility be avoided, Judge Richardson had discreetly made up his mind to accept the inevitable. Instead of opposing the plan, therefore, his reply suggested what seemed to him the best way to accomplish its purpose. It was not to disturb the two courts of probate and of insolvency, but to abolish the offices of the judges, and then provide for the appointment of one judge of probate and insolvency in each county, who should *ex-officio* be judge of both courts. By this method of procedure the business of the two courts would be kept entirely separate. To be sure, a question of the constitutionality of the project at once presented itself; and while to many of those who had considered the subject it appeared to be a matter of more or less doubt, Judge Richardson, always extremely cautious when projecting the draft of a statute, himself felt confident upon that point, and so assured the committee.

The plan thus recommended by Judge Richardson was finally adopted. A bill drawn up by Chairman Stone was reported, abolishing the offices of judge of probate and judge of insolvency in each county, and establishing the office of judge of probate and insolvency. This bill and the address to the governor stood upon the legislative calendar at the same time. The friends of the two measures had each determined to get their own bill up first, for neither wanted to vote against the other; besides, if the consolidation bill should first pass, the address would be useless.

The remainder of the narrative may be told in Judge Richardson's own words :

The address was a little ahead, came to a vote and was passed. After much debate, the consolidation bill then came up and went through without opposition. This turned out of office twenty-seven judges, two in each of thirteen counties, and one judge of probate in the very small county of Dukes, where he had done the business of both offices for some years. Then came the appointments, which were announced a month or two afterwards. Banks was governor, and he promptly removed Loring, though he had been opposed to that way of getting rid of him. Still he found it necessary to accede to public opinion, unlike his predecessor, Governor Gardner, who had refused to do so the year before.

I had not voted for Banks at the preceding election, and he knew it. I voted for Gardner, who had twice honored me with appointments, although I had not voted for him at his first election. I belonged to the old whig party, and followed its fortunes until it expired with the defeat of Governor Washburn, in 1854, by the election of Governor Gardner. Parties were in a transition state, and men voted as they pleased without much reference to party ties, except the Democrats, who never faltered. There seemed little chance for me at the hands of Governor Banks. But when the appointments were announced I was named judge of probate and insolvency for Middlesex. Of the twenty-seven judges only four were re-appointed, two probate and two insolvency judges, and nine new men were brought out. I was one of the fortunate few.

For the more convenient prosecution of business, Judge Richardson, in 1860, removed his law office from Lowell to Boston, and took up a residence in Cambridge. Here for nearly ten years he pursued the even tenor of his way, regular and punctual in attendance at court, where, free from distractions, he dispatched each day's business with ease and rapidity. One might say of him that he was "content, because all things were to his liking."

At this point a word or two may be permitted with regard to the political and religious tenets of the subject of this sketch. Judge Richardson was originally (as his father had been before him) a whig, and by natural transition he became a republican. In saying this, the writer is not unmindful of that small fraction of the whig party in Massachusetts, pro-slavery in sentiment, who, after the death of Webster and the disruption of the whig party, found themselves in the democratic camp. Judge Richardson was not a partisan, but he held firm political convictions, and gave his unswerving adherence to the doctrines of the republican faith. Regardful of the proprieties of the bench, however, he abstained from mingling in party politics. When the rebellion came, it found him intensely loyal to the cause of the Union, and in fullest sympathy with the public utterances and acts of Abraham Lincoln.

It used to be good-naturedly said of Judge Story, that so fixed were his views upon religious subjects, and so hearty his belief in his own church, that, with rare exuberance of spirit, whenever he met a stranger and the conversation reverted to the topic of religion, he, unless informed to the contrary, took it for granted

that his companion was a Unitarian. Judge
Richardson did not go to this length. Indeed, he
rarely discussed the subject of any man's belief,
or of attendance upon public worship. He was
a Unitarian, and at Washington was an active
and valued member of a church of that denomination, where he was esteemed as a man of good
works, as well as of liberal belief.* It may be said
of Judge Richardson that alike in politics and
religion, he entertained decided views, but he
enjoyed them in serenity, and with no desire to
impose them upon others.

The career of the American lawyer who sticks
to his profession is for the most part uneventful;
and the life we have had under review has thus
far flowed with a smooth current. The labor of
the bench proving to his taste Judge Richardson
had reason to look forward in the ordinary course
of events to a long continuance in office. But
fate had willed it otherwise. Without previous
warning, he who above others felt himself bound
by strong ties to home and familiar scenes, was
called upon to put off the judicial robe and enter
into a field of public service, of a character wholly
different from that to which he had hitherto been
accustomed.

When General Grant had taken the oath of

---

* All Souls', of which for many years he was a trustee. One of the
most beautiful windows of stained glass in the country is that in memory
of Mrs. Richardson, placed in that church in 1881, by her husband.

office for his first term as President of the United
States, he treated the country, it may be recalled,
to a genuine surprise by sending to the Senate
the name of A. T. Stewart, of New York, to be
Secretary of the Treasury. Hardly had the news
of the President's choice gone to the country,
when somebody discovered that Mr. Stewart,
being in trade, was disqualified under the law.
Withdrawing the nomination, the President substituted a name at the announcement of which
the people were as much gratified as they had
before been astonished. Notwithstanding that he
had already taken one member of the cabinet
from Massachusetts, the President honored that
state still further by selecting for the treasury,
George Sewall Boutwell, one of the ablest of
a distinguished line of statesmen sent by the
Commonwealth to Congress, or elevated to the
position of her chief magistracy. It is enough to
say of Governor Boutwell that the reputation
earned by his long and varied public service,
gave assurance to the country that the grave
question of our financial policy,—the problem of
the hour,—would be wisely solved by him, a
confidence indeed that subsequent events amply
sustained.

A resident of Groton since 1835, Boutwell had
been from that date a warm personal friend of
Judge Richardson. That he accepted the Treas-

ury, yielding after a brief time only for deliberation, was in part because his mind had reverted
to his friend on the bench in Middlesex, as the
man of all others that he wanted for assistant
secretary. President Grant had, as it were, impressed Governor Boutwell into service, and the
latter in turn literally reached out for the Massachusetts judge to come to his help. The first
intimation to Judge Richardson that he was
needed reached him in the shape of a telegram
from the new Secretary of the Treasury, asking if
he would accept the office of assistant secretary.
He hastened to Washington, and after a protracted
consultation between the two friends, his consent,
most reluctantly yielded, was given to take the
position for the time being. This occurred near
the end of March, 1869.

Meanwhile a vacancy happening on the bench
of the superior court of the state, Governor Claflin, unwilling that the services of such a man
should be lost to Massachusetts, tendered the
appointment to Judge Richardson. The honor
was declined, upon the earnest protest of the Secretary of the Treasury, although the Governor had
proceeded so far as to make out the commission.

The post of assistant secretary of the Treasury,
at the head of a force of officers and clerks which
numbered in Washington alone nearly twenty-
two hundred persons, was, it may well be imag-

ined, no sinecure. It offered a certainty of hard work, to be kept up without cessation. This prospect, however, rather attracted Judge Richardson than otherwise. That his duty, as it seemed to him, plainly lay at home, accounts for the extreme reluctance which marked his tarrying at Washington. As a matter of fact, while day after day went by, he attempted more than once to resign, but his repeated resignations were disregarded. Meanwhile, he retained the office of judge of probate and insolvency of Middlesex, expecting before long to be at home in Cambridge.

The unusual character of his entry upon administrative duties at Washington is noted here in order that the reader may the more completely enter into the spirit of generosity and friendship with which Secretary Boutwell alludes to this interesting period of their joint career. In an address of mingled force and feeling, delivered before the Court of Claims, upon the occasion of the proceedings in memory of the Chief Justice, the distinguished ex-Secretary, having dwelt upon the reluctance of his friend to come to Washington, observes:

After a delay of several months, he yielded to my importunities, but against his own inclinations, and thus entered a larger field of public service.

In the three and a half years of our association, he contributed largely to whatever of success was attained during my administration of the Treasury Department.*

---

*Appendix, post, p. xlv.

It will thus be seen that in consenting to take upon himself the burden of an office, new to his experience, the assistant was admitted to the fullest confidence of his chief. The two rejoiced not only in the harmony of a close friendship, but in the growth that comes from daily contact of one superior mind with another while dealing with subjects of large concern, and breathing the free atmosphere of high, intellectual endeavor.

Whatever diversity of opinion may prevail as to the wisdom of the policy adopted by Secretary Chase of issuing paper money to carry on the war, it gave birth at least to one chapter of our financial history that excites nothing but admiration. The resolve of the people to maintain at the highest possible standard the credit of the United States, while bearing the burden of an enormous war debt, won for them the respect of the world. It is of course impossible to ascribe to any one man, or set of men, the credit for this sound public sentiment; yet there were leaders of political thought to whom special honor is due for advancing and unflinchingly maintaining correct and hopeful views, whence came the impetus that ended in legislation appropriate to this desired end. Of these eminent men no one stands deservedly higher in public esteem than George S. Boutwell.

The debt of the United States when largest

(1 March, 1866) stood at the enormous figures of $2,707,856,000.22. Such was the legacy left to the American people by the war for the Union. The original legal-tender act, in its title, was an authority for "the issue of notes and the redemption and funding thereof," and it provided for the funding of the floating debt of the United States. It required that duties on imported goods should be paid in coin, and that such coin should be set apart as a special fund, first for the payment in coin of the interest on the bonds and notes of the United States; and next for the purchase or payment of one per centum of the entire debt of the United States, to be made within each fiscal year after the 1st of July, 1862, this to be set apart as a sinking fund, and the interest thereon, in a like manner, to be applied to the purchase or payment of the public debt as the Secretary of the Treasury should direct. While war was flagrant, the government struggling for existence was still borrowing money to pay old loans, and creating new ones, so that no steps were taken to establish a sinking fund as such. Coin in the Treasury, however, was allowed to accumulate to the amount of about $100,000,000.

President Grant in his inaugural address, 4 March, 1869, employed this significant language:

A great debt has been contracted in securing to us and to our posterity the Union. The payment of this, principal and interest, as well as the return to a specie basis, as soon as it can be accomplished without material detriment to the labor classes, or to the country at large, must be provided for.

A prompt yet safely conducted reduction of the public debt* was the key-note of Secretary Boutwell's administration. To this end with a firm and inflexible purpose he bent his energies. He meant that not a single item of taxation should be prematurely given up, but that the country should practice economy and devote every dollar it could save to the payment of its bonds. He set at once to work to begin the creation of an actual sinking fund, in literal compliance with the law of Congress, hitherto neglected. He proposed a plan for funding the national debt which Congress sanctioned and embodied in the important legislation of 14 July, 1870, enabling the Secretary to fund in new securities at a lower rate of interest, that part of the national debt represented by five-twenty bonds. †

Although to one looking back upon its successful execution, the plan may now appear perfectly simple and easy, it in truth represented at the time the result of anxious thought, a courageous faith, and the exercise of sound judgment. Gold, at that period, it should be

---

* The public debt, 1 March, 1869, was $2,525,463,260.01, a reduction of about $180,000,000 from the highest point it had ever reached.

† So-called because redeemable at the pleasure of the United States after five years, and payable twenty years from date. They were first issued in 1862 ; and they bore six per cent. interest, payable semi-annually.

remembered, still commanded a premium; and there were many who insisted that resumption of specie payments could not be accomplished, and that it was only a delusion to believe that the war debt of the United States would ever be extinguished.

Now that the policy of the government had taken shape, it remained for the Secretary of the Treasury to accomplish the business of disposing of the new five per cents. This was a task of no little magnitude. The previous season, owing to the Franco-Prussian war, was unfavorable for placing a loan of the United States abroad; and that branch of the work had to be temporarily deferred. Meanwhile, at the request of the Secretary, the amount of the five per cents had been increased by Congress from $200,000,000 to $500,000,000, and a discretion had been conferred upon him to make the interest payable quarter-yearly. The assistant secretary entered zealously into the spirit of the enterprise. He was active in letter writing and in personal conference with leading bankers and capitalists, where he displayed a thorough knowledge of the needs of the government, and of the capacity of private individuals, firms and corporations to take the loan, and showed likewise a keen insight into the practical workings of the money market. As illustrating with what clearness of vision he surveyed the situation, the following extract may be cited, from a letter of his to the Secretary of the Treasury, 17 March, 1871, reporting the result of an interview on that day in New York city with certain prominent bankers :

I can see the reason they want me here, which I did not understand at first. They are all deeply engaged in other matters ; they can not be got together unless it is to *meet somebody ;* and when they do get together they are all in a hurry to get away, and all talk at the same time, and they want some one to bring order out of the chaos of their discussions and to sum up the general conclusions, which I have done as well as I am able. As you take up the matter where I leave off I trust you will not think their conclusions were reached at once and were discussed afterwards. I think it is a decided advantage that you can consider these propositions from an entirely different standpoint from that of the parties who discussed them, and from that of myself who heard them discussed.

The Secretary had caused public announcement to be made in February, 1871, that on the 6th of March following books would be opened in this country and in Europe for subscriptions, the first preference being given to subscribers for the five per cents. By the first of August nearly sixty-six millions had been taken, chiefly by the national banks, leaving one hundred and thirty-four millions to be disposed of in Europe, with such added subscriptions at home as might reasonably be counted upon at that advanced stage of the business.

The banking house of Jay Cooke & Company,

confident of their ability to place the loan, had undertaken to obtain subscriptions for this large amount, the bonds to be delivered on the first day of December, 1871. The house was not however an agent of the government under any specified authority. Upon making subscriptions each subscriber was to pay down five per cent. on the sum, which amount was to be applied to the payment of the principal of the bonds when the same were delivered; if the subscriber was disinclined to take the bonds, the five per cent. became forfeited to the banking firm.

At that season, it should be understood, the house of Jay Cooke & Company was a strong one, full of resources. Their energy practically brought about the result at which they had aimed, namely, a disposition of the whole of the remaining amount of the five per cents, almost all of which was placed abroad. The new bonds had to be shipped to London, and could be delivered to Jay Cooke & Company there upon payment by them in gold, or by delivery of an equal amount of five-twenties, both sets of bonds being reckoned at their respective par values.

The tremendous responsibility of handling these new bonds rested upon Secretary Boutwell. Of course, he had to trust somebody with their actual custody and delivery in a foreign country. The one man whom he knew that he could rely

upon to discharge efficiently this duty was close
at hand. He selected the assistant secretary,
though a temporary absence of that officer from
his post would be severely felt at the Treasury.

Another duty not less grave, and one that required for its successful performance much tact
and delicacy, was to examine the ground, both in
England and upon the continent, with reference
to negotiating a similar loan at four and a-half
per cent. It is no exaggeration to say that for
this office, at the period named, no one of a fitness superior to Judge Richardson could have
been suggested.

Plans were concluded for the safe transportation to London of the new securities, and for the
redemption thereby of the five-twenties for which
a call had been issued. A clerical force having
been specially selected and arrangements completed for their transportation, Assistant Secretary Richardson, accompanied by Mr. J. P. Bigelow, chief of the loan division, sailed from New
York on the 14th of June. They went directly
through to London.

Upon arrival, the assistant secretary lost no
time in securing proper quarters. His object
was to occupy rooms in close proximity to the
banks, and yet wholly apart from any banking-
house. Quarters were finally obtained at 41 Lombard street, in the City, a locality that may be

described as the actual financial centre of the world. Here the clerks, provided with ledgers and other conveniences for keeping accounts and carrying on, under proper checks, the business of issuing bonds, and buying and cancelling bonds that had been redeemed, were ready to work out the details of the important transaction for which they had been brought across the water. It was to all intents and purposes a branch of the Treasury of the United States, opened at London.

The new bonds were in condition for shipment, and were sent from the Treasury on the first of September. Three clerks, in whom the department imposed a more than usual confidence, were given charge of a safe containing the bonds, whose value ran up into the millions. These men were armed. Not for one moment from the time the safe left the Treasury building in Washington (except while in the "strong room" of a Cunard steamer) until it was delivered to Assistant Secretary Richardson in person, at the branch office in London was the precious object out of the sight of at least two of these government officials. Similar precautions were observed in shipping home the bonds which were received in exchange; and in fact whenever it became necessary to take securities across the ocean.

The Treasury Department could know only in a general way how large was the volume of the coupon bonds of the United States held in Europe. What amount was owned in England, what in Germany and what in Holland, it was impossible to determine. Besides, it was not easy to get word to holders that their bonds had been called, and it resulted that while a very large proportion quickly reached London for redemption, much remained outstanding. On 17 September, 1871, the assistant secretary of the Treasury had in his possession at London $30,000,000 of the new five per cent. bonds.

His first action was to sell outright a portion of them, for which he received gold. This gold he placed on deposit in the Bank of England,* and with it he was ready to pay such holders of 5-20's as preferred to receive in exchange money rather than new bonds. The amount called was $100,000,000, and interest ceased 1 December, 1871. From a report of the Secretary of the Treasury of that date we learn that the department had in its possession 1 December, 1871, more than $80,000,000 of the bonds. Of these, $17,000,000 had been paid in coin, while the

---

* Not a little difficulty was experienced by him in arranging this deposit so as to conform to the rules of the Bank of England, and at the same time render it possible for him to draw out the money upon his own check. The solution of this problem will be found described in a report from Assistant Secretary Richardson to Secretary Boutwell, which is printed in the Appendix, *post*. At one time there was on the books of the Bank standing to the credit of the assistant secretary more money than had ever been on deposit to the credit of any one man since the Bank was created.

remainder had been received on deposit in exchange for five per cents.

The business once set in operation went on
with a considerable degree of regularity. The
clerks worked willingly, sometimes far beyond
the usual office hours. The supply of bonds for
redemption, as already intimated, varied in
amount so that at some seasons the work to be
accomplished was greater than at others.

The mission entrusted to Assistant Secretary
Richardson, as we have seen, was such as to test
his ability not only as an executive officer, but as
a diplomat, so to speak, in finance. To distribute
by safe and expeditious process an enormous
amount of public securities already bespoken,
constitutes in itself a work that few men are
qualified to prosecute. But to go further, and
while engrossed in this work to watch closely the
field of European finance, with a view of placing
most advantageously another loan at a lower rate
of interest; to measure the capacities, and to overcome the prejudices of the great bankers of England and of the Continent,—this indeed was to tax
the powers of the most astute and experienced
leader in public financial affairs. Herein Judge
Richardson displayed talent of a rare order. At
each step he proved himself alert, keenly observant,
and to a remarkable degree sagacious.

He appears to have sought from the beginning

by all available means to enlarge the circle of
persons abroad who were really influential, and
whom it was desirable to acquaint with the
nature of our securities. His methods were far-
sighted. He labored to inculcate a belief in the
stability of our government, and in the certainty
that our indebtedness would be paid dollar for
dollar. Above all he kept steadily in view the
fact that, with credit improving, we could borrow
at a lower rate of interest. He contrived to meet
in person and talk with the heads of the great
banking houses. At these interviews, his attitude was that of a man having something to sell,
which the prospective customer wanted to get as
cheaply as possible. It was a prime requisite
that the official representing the United States
should be able to feel sure of his ground, by
reason of his complete apprehension of the
financial situation. So far as one may ascertain,
from papers, official and otherwise, bearing upon
the subject, this requirement was amply met.

The reader ought to be reminded that although
the United States, from the day that the war
closed, had caused it to be made known that
their obligations would be paid dollar for dollar,
and had in proof of good faith gone on diminish-
ing the amount of the indebtedness, still so vast
was the total that the credit abroad of the
government, while in the main good, was by

some banking firms held under suspicion. The financial editor of the *Times*, for example, did not hesitate to inform the representative of the Treasury that, for his part, he did not consider as quite safe the loan of any country governed by universal suffrage. One of the great money kings, whose name if disclosed would be recognized the world over, though proffering social advances, and treating the assistant secretary with all proper respect, could scarcely conceal from him a profound sense of hostility to the loan. Not only this, the members of his banking-house were actually discouraging investors from purchasing our new bonds. The house, it seems, was then devoting much attention to the French loan, and Judge Richardson was favored with the remark, "Of course, everybody would prefer a French bond to an American one at the same price."

Nor had the treaty of Washington, with its avowed purpose of healing enmities between England and America and of bringing the two countries into closer accord, the effect in the slightest to render our securities popular among the banks and the investors of London. One reason why money lenders in England were not disposed to look with favor upon large purchases of United States securities was because of the great losses suffered by many who, eager for large

dividends, had invested in the Erie railroad.
This corporation, it will be remembered, through
the management of Fisk and Gould, had brought
into public notice abroad the uncertainty, to say
the least, of investments in an American bonded
debt. Government bonds of the United States
suffered because Englishmen had lost money
which they had put into the securities of a
private American corporation.

These facts are laid before the reader in order
that he may possess a proper sense of the obstacles
with which Judge Richardson had to contend.
After having exchanged views with the represen-
tatives of the great houses in London, he visited,
on a like errand, Amsterdam, Frankfort-on-the-
Main, Hamburg, and Paris. At each of these
cities, in his capacity as representative of the
Government of the United States, he met the
leading men who controlled financial operations,
and talked with them in explanation of what
the United States expected to accomplish. He
appears to have acquired a wholesome respect
for Dutch bankers, esteeming their capacities as
much in advance of those of the heads of the
great banking houses in London. He frequently
dined out, and was the recipient of numerous
social attentions, quietly taking the measure
all the while of the men whom he met, and
their power to control large sums of money. Of

one of these bankers, for instance, he remarks, "I was with him a good deal, dined with him, and talked much about our bonds and investments generally. Socially, I liked him very much, but financially, I found him of no account whatever."

Then, too, he noted and made due allowance for the inevitable jealousies and heated rivalry that his presence in Europe upon such a mission could not but engender. To add to his responsibilities, there were one or two Americans, of foreign birth, with whom he had to deal, individuals who affected to know precisely how funding operations should be carried on, and who were free in their criticism of the policy of the administration. These men took pains to have it understood that they were foreign correspondents of influential journals in the United States. In what Judge Richardson said, and still more in what he omitted to say, to all such persons, it is known that he acted with admirable tact and discretion.

His reports, both official and private, to the Secretary of the Treasury show that he was easily master of the situation. He counted upon returning home, where he much wished to be; but there was more for him to do, and consequently his return was, with his cheerful assent, postponed until spring. He speaks of meeting persons of character and standing almost daily

who desired to talk with him in relation to our
national debt, the new loan and the resources of
the country, as well as the policy of the administration. To all who sought it he could furnish
information, in full detail, better perhaps than
any other man who might have been sent abroad.
He says:

> I am sowing the seeds, the fruits of which to some small
> extent are seen and will continue to be seen more and more
> in the increased popularity of our new loan, at reduced rates
> of interest, among the investors of England.

The governor of the Bank of England, for example, after expressing the greatest admiration
for the policy of the United States, in regularly
and largely reducing the national debt, admitted
to the assistant secretary that—

> Until lately he had always thought that the debt could
> not be reduced, but it had been shown that the resources of
> the country were so enormous, and the determination of the
> nation to pay the debt so fixed and settled, we should now be
> able to borrow money at four per cent.

In acquainting the Secretary of the Treasury
with the circumstances of this interview, the judge
adds shrewdly:

> I can not help believing that the fact of your having some
> three millions pounds sterling here in London, for which the
> government appears to have no immediate use, has con-
> tributed no little in the mind of the governor and the directors
> of the Bank of England, and others who know it, to strengthen
> the credit of the United States in this great metropolis.

We pass over the details of his stay to mention one occurrence of striking import. There are many now living who can recall vividly the intense excitement that seized upon the English press and people over the prospect of "the indirect claims" for the depredations of the Confederate cruisers being made the subject of action by the tribunal at Geneva, under the treaty of Washington. Perhaps no single event in recent British political history, of interest to Americans, is more striking than the suddenness and depth of the popular feeling in England which threatened to wreck the treaty and postpone the settlement of the Alabama claims.

Judge Richardson went through this tempest with calmness and with a perfectly clear vision. He did not in the least degree misconceive the impression made upon the English people of all classes of society, or exaggerate its importance. Writing in February, 1872, he says:

It is astonishing what a scare this case has made in England. People are fearfully alarmed lest there should be war. All hopes of any further negotiations of the funded loan until this scare is over must be abandoned, but it enables me to buy old bonds. I have bought largely for delivery by the middle of February, and I think by the middle of March, if not sooner, I shall have invested all the money I shall have received. The last million of bonds sent over will not be sold unless there is a great change in public sentiment.

One of the first results of the fright at the spectre of the indirect claims was, as the judge remarks, to send down, in the London market, the price of our bonds. It would be interesting to know, if some genius at figures were to work out the problem, how much was saved to the United States Treasury by this depreciation for the time being in our securities.

Assistant Secretary Richardson did not return home until early in the spring of 1872, reaching New York in the "China" of the Cunard line, and bringing home the books and official records. The last instalment of $12,000,000 of retired bonds arrived in New York about the same time by another steamer. The system which he had established was continued; and the way once opened the work was kept up with more or less fluctuation, according to the course of events, tending to advance or depress the market price at London of the securities of the United States.

An interesting outcome of the successful placing of this loan was the complete change of tone that ensued on the part of English bankers. The very individuals who had expressed in such positive terms their conviction of the precarious nature of the securities of the United States were now entertaining an entirely different opinion. An animated demand for the bonds began to spring up in every direction. The power and the perfect good faith of the United States had been most satisfactorily demonstrated. No small share in this success may, with propriety, be credited, and indeed ought to be credited, to the faithful services of the quiet, modest representative of the Treasury, whom Secretary Boutwell had sent abroad. From that time onward no difficulty whatever has been experienced in Europe in disposing of any portion of our public loan.

Immediately after arriving at Washington, he resigned his probate judgeship, thus settling for the time being at least, the question of his stay at the Capital. In a letter 11 April, 1872, to the governor of Massachusetts (Washburn), he says:

With great attachment for the county of my birth, and the people among whom I have always lived, my own preference has been and still is, to remain in the position in Massachusetts which I have held so many years; but on returning to Washington at this time, I have been induced, contrary to my own inclination, to continue for some time longer as assistant secretary of the Treasury; and now, having decided upon that course, I prefer to forward to you my resignation.

The retention of a judicial office during so long a period of absence from the State was, to say the least, somewhat out of the usual course. It is however readily explained. When dispatched abroad he had been given to understand that his labors would be required there for a brief season only. He looked forward to a speedy accomplishment of the object of the mission, and a return to his home at Cambridge, where official labors were so much to his taste. But upon his reaching Washington, he was persuaded that the familiarity he had now acquired of the workings of the Treasury Department, and the invaluable experience gained by his stay in Europe combined to make it his plain duty to remain at the post of assistant secretary.

In the campaign of 1872, the Republicans stood as a unit in their determination to nominate President Grant for a second term. They selected as candidate for vice-president, Henry Wilson, at that time senator from Massachusetts. The election of Grant and Wilson by an unprecedented majority showed how strong was the hold of the Republican party upon the country, and how great was the confidence of the people in the integrity and wisdom of General Grant. Soon after the election it became apparent that Massachusetts would send Secretary Boutwell to the Senate for Wilson's unexpired term. Knowledge of this purpose evoked a curiosity more than usually active as to who should succeed to the Treasury. Those who had closely watched the current of events, and who knew how firm was the President in his friendships, had no great difficulty in determining for them-

selves who was the man that he had in mind.
It was a well-known trait of General Grant,
exhibited both in his military and civil career,
that he attached himself warmly to his intimates,
and that he stood by a friend with admirable con-
stancy. Already the President had come to know
and highly esteem Assistant Secretary Richardson.
The names of Governor Morgan and of Messrs.
Cisco and Clews, were brought forward by the
press of New York city as those of whom one
was likely to receive the appointment. It is
doubtful, however, whether the President ever
conceived the idea of appointing any other person than Richardson, who was in fact appointed
17 March, 1873.*

Many bankers, capitalists and business men of
New York city were very urgent in their commendation of one or more of the gentlemen
named, for the reason that what had come to be
known as the "Boutwell policy" was not entirely
to their liking. There existed more or less dis-
trust of the secretary, on the ground that he
took too lax a view of the power of the President to issue treasury notes up to the limit of
$400,000,000. While it was wholly without
foundation, there was yet a belief that Secretary

---

*The Cabinet consisted as follows:
Hamilton Fish, *State;* William W. Belknap, *War;* William A. Rich-
ardson, *Treasury;* George M. Robeson, *Navy;* John J. Creswell, *Post Office;*
Columbus Delano, *Interior;* George H. Williams, *Attorney General.*

Boutwell, and those who thought with him, were too partial to paper money. Such a feeling could but add to the insistence with which the names of New York candidates were brought forward and urged upon the President.

We have just seen how reluctant was the subject of this sketch to lay down judicial office, and apply himself to national administrative work. The same considerations of duty that determined him to forego his own choice and remain at Washington, were not without their force when the question of promotion to be Secretary of the Treasury presented itself. That the honor and the prestige of the high office carried great weight with Judge Richardson, it is idle to deny. Nor should it be intimated that the offer of a seat in the cabinet found him other than willing to accept the distinction. It deserves to be said, however, that the place was not sought by him, nor was it taken as a reward of ambition.

President Grant liked Secretary Richardson; and the appointment brought with it the mingled pleasure of a promotion for public service well rendered, and a token of personal friendship and esteem. The condition of the public finances at this particular time must have gone far to influence the new secretary in his decision to remain at Washington. At a later day, speaking of the period of his accession to the Treasury, he characterized the situation as being "the worst time in the worst condition of things that ever existed under any secretary."

He had been identified, as we have seen, with the successful conduct of funding operations abroad; and as these were to be continued, he must to some extent have felt an obligation (when so invited) to remain at the side of the President until that great work had been carried nearer to completion. Again, it is to be observed that Judge Richardson had some prescience of the financial trouble that lay ahead, a consciousness that appealed to him to stand by the President, and vindicate the soundness of the plans which Secretary Boutwell with the aid of his assistant secretary had set in operation. In a letter to Boutwell, President Grant had said (and the country was glad to hear it) that with the new Secretary of the Treasury there would be "no departure" from the financial policy of his predecessor. There was a certain sense of relief in the assurance that a man of experience and a close friend of Secretary Boutwell was to continue at the head of the Treasury. Still, it should be added that in certain quarters the promotion met with no little opposition and criticism. There were those who, while freely admitting that the assistant secretary had admirably done his part, were apprehensive that a like measure of success might not attend his elevation to a post, exacting in its many grave duties, and compelling him to take upon himself the entire responsibility.

Much has been written of the radical social changes wrought by the war for the Union. Prominent among these changes, and one perhaps the most to be deplored, may be reckoned an increasing love of display, extending in some instances to a lavish and therefore vulgar expenditure of wealth. So far as such a tendency to deterioration in national character was to be attributed to the disturbing influence of the sudden acquisition of large fortunes in war times, it has no doubt, in fact, been checked by a return to peace, as well as by the good sense of the American people. A lingering effect of this false estimate of the uses of money was perceptible, however, at the Capital for many years after the war had closed.

The assertion had come to be frequently made, and in some quarters acquiesced in, that a cabinet officer ought to spend the greater part of his salary in social entertainment. The amount of salary at present paid to a cabinet officer, it must be admitted, is none too large; in fact one may well doubt whether it be sufficient for a proper discharge of the duties of the position. At all events, it is very generally understood that a public man can ill afford to take a seat in the cabinet, without having at least a respectable income of his own beyond what the salary yields.

Secretary Richardson, though not wealthy, met in a generous spirit all the social obligations of his official rank and station. While not specially fond of society, he did not fail to recognize the advantage to the administration of entertaining upon the scale that had become customary, and that in one sense the world had a right to expect. He took a large and handsome house on H street between Fourteenth and Fifteenth streets known as the "Kennedy house," and celebrated in years gone by for its scenes of hospitality. Here Mrs. Richardson and her daughter welcomed the visitor, and won for the secretary the reputation of possessing one of the most attractive homes in Washington.

A commendable trait of him, the events of whose public life we are rapidly passing in review, was his modest and unaffected bearing in office, and his abstention from seeking popular applause. Of course Secretary Richardson had a desire to stand well in public esteem—what right-minded servant of the people has not?—but he spurned everything like notoriety, and did nothing consciously from a motive of attracting favorable attention. When he could, he preferred to do his work quietly and unobserved, letting the

public learn that the work was accomplished as
their first intimation that he had been engaged
in doing it.

An instance of his carrying through to success
a highly important undertaking, and yet dispens-
ing with any "flourish of trumpets" about it, is
seen in the circumstances attending the method,
originated and carried out by him, to effect the
payment by Great Britain of the fifteen and a half
millions of dollars in gold coin that she was obliged
to pay by the terms of the award, in 1872, of the
Geneva Tribunal. The plan was happily conceived. The whole business was most creditable to
the secretary, yet he treated it as a simple matter
that came along in the routine of work, and said
nothing about it until ten years later, when he
was asked to write out a narrative of the transaction as an event of historic interest.

The money, which would weigh twenty-eight
and a half tons in coin, by the terms of the
treaty had to be paid within a year from the
third of September, 1872. Naturally the expectation of moving so large a sum from London to
New York caused anxiety among business men
and bankers, lest a financial disturbance, created
thereby, might seriously affect and disturb exchange and business relations generally between
this country and Europe. To effect a payment quietly and almost without observation

was a task peculiarly congenial to Secretary Richardson. He adopted and successfully put into operation the following ingenious method of transferring this extraordinarily large sum without danger and without disturbing in the slightest degree the business interests of the two countries.

As we are already aware, the Treasury Department at this period was engaged in the business of calling in for redemption the six per cent. bonds of the United States, and paying therefor with the proceeds of the sale of the five per cent. bonds of the funded loan under the act of July 4, 1870. The agency instituted at London for this purpose had been in successful operation, and the work was being prosecuted without the least difficulty or disturbance.

The Secretary of the Treasury availed himself of the existence of this office in London to effect the payment of the fifteen and a half millions in gold coin. He called on the 6th of June, 1873, for the redemption of twenty millions of 5-20 six per cent. bonds of the loan of 1862. But fifteen and a half millions of this were required, but experience had shown that a certain percentage of the amount called for did not respond, owing to the fact that holders lacking the information, or for some other reason, would defer action until long after the maturity of the call.

Nearly all the coupon bonds of this loan of

1862 were held in Europe, and could be purchased in the London market. Accompanying the issue of the call were instructions, which were forwarded to the Treasury agents in London, that if parties desired to deposit at the agency called bonds or matured coupons (practically the same as coin) to the credit of persons in the United States, to be applied in payment of money payable to the United States, on or after the time of the maturity of the call of that date, the agents might receive such bonds or coupons, telegraphing from time to time the amount and the names of the parties to whose credit they had been deposited. The agents were then to cancel and forward to the Treasury Department at Washington, just as soon as possible, such bonds and coupons as they should receive. They were directed not to mingle in any way the account of these bonds and coupons with the receipt of those in connection with their funding operations. The amounts payable on account of such deposits were to be accounted for and settled by the Treasury of the United States at Washington.

It will be seen that these specific instructions had in mind the receipt and cancellation of at least fifteen millions and a half of bonds, for the purpose of paying the Geneva award money.

At the same time the parties who were understood to be employed by the British government to make this transfer, and the public likewise, were notified of these instructions. As early as June, therefore, certain parties began to buy called bonds and matured coupons, and turn them over to the United States Treasury agents in London. Before the date for the payment of the award, these parties had deposited in the Treasury of the United States, either directly or through the London agency, the whole fifteen and a half million dollars. They had taken coin certificates in different sums from time to time as they made the deposits, instead of drawing the coin from the Treasury in payment.

All these certificates were returned and cancelled 9 September, 1873, and one coin certificate for the full amount of fifteen and a half million dollars was issued to the depositors and made payable to their order. They were Drexel, Morgan & Company, Morton, Bliss & Company, and Jay Cooke & Company. These bankers endorsed the certificate "to the joint order of H. B. M. Minister, or *Chargé-d'Affaires* at Washington, and Acting Consul-General at New York." These officials, Sir Edward Thornton, then minister, and Mr. Archibald, consul-general, endorsed the certificate to the order of Hamilton Fish, Secretary of State. Mr. Fish added his endorsement, "Pay to the order of Honorable William A. Richardson, Secretary of the Treasury."

The Secretary of the Treasury, upon receiving this certificate, proceeded to carry out the provisions of the act of 3 March, 1873, providing that as soon as the money should be paid it should be used to redeem, as far as it might, the public debt; for the amount of the debt so redeemed, the act said, should be invested in the five per cent. registered bonds of the United States, to be subject to the future disposition of Congress.

Secretary Richardson, accordingly, issued to the Secretary of State one five per cent. registered bond of the funded loan, for fifteen millions and a half of dollars. Of course, there was no engraved bond for that amount that could be used. In order, however, to carry out the purposes of the act in harmony with the issues of registered bonds generally, the Secretary had a special design made of a bond, elegantly written, with suitable ornamentation and border. It followed the system of numbering and was registered as Bond No. 1 of that denomination.*

" Thus you see," says the chief justice, writing of this transaction in 1882, " that the whole business was done without the payment of actual coin into the Treasury. The bonds and coupons in Europe were bought up with money paid there, not by the United States Government, and together with those deposited here, were redeemed without the payment of

---

* Credit for this fine piece of work is due to Edwin B. MacGrotty, a clerk in the division of loans and currency, who was an expert penman. Mr. MacGrotty to-day (September, 1898) is in the division of book-keeping and warrants of the Treasury.

money, but by the issue of coin certificates, which were paid
or redeemed in a bond of the funded loan.

"The transaction was carried on so gradually, extending
over a period of three months, that its effect upon exchange
or business was too insignificant to attract notice of any kind,
if indeed it had any effect whatever one way or the other."

The panic of 1873 will long be remembered.
Bankers and merchants one after another failed,
and the business of the country received a shock
from which it took years to recover. The crisis
was inevitable. Corporations, firms and individuals had gone heavily in debt. Speculation
was at its height. Although securities of almost
every description enjoyed a high nominal value, a
protracted course of over-trading had brought
business generally into a condition of imminent
peril. The crash came. A season of fright
ensued when all eyes were turned to the President and the Secretary of the Treasury. Help
was implored of them. Their response was
just what it should have been—a calm, judicious
announcement, based upon a strict adherence to
law. The events of that momentous period, as
may well be imagined, form a most striking
chapter in the public experiences of Secretary
Richardson.

On Thursday, 18 September, 1873, the banking
house of Jay Cooke & Company, of Philadelphia,
which had become closely identified with the
Northern Pacific Railroad, suddenly suspended.

Immediately the First National Bank of Washington shut its doors, and other financial institutions intimately connected with Jay Cooke & Company, in various parts of the country, did the like. The news spread like wildfire, and universal disaster was threatened. In this emergency the weak and failing bankers and business men looked for aid to the Treasury of the United States. This was the place above all others where they never should have looked, for the Treasury had its full share of burdens to preserve the public credit in the general crash. But the sentiment in New York city was very strong that somehow the government ought to come to the rescue. Many of the bankers there knew President Grant personally, and some of them were his warm friends.

The cry was that the Secretary should at once issue the reserve, and by this means ease the money market. At that time there was in the Treasury a reserve fund of forty-four millions of United States Treasury notes, or "greenbacks," as they were popularly called. The total amount that Congress had authorized to be issued was four hundred millions. The law had required the Secretary to retire this amount from circulation gradually. The process of retiring had been entered upon, when by a later act Congress had stopped it, leaving three hundred and fifty-six

millions in circulation. The forty-four millions
difference, received and cancelled at the Treasury,
was the subject of an almost endless contention
as to whether the Secretary of the Treasury
had the authority under the law as it then
stood to re-issue it or any part of it. Secretary
Boutwell conceived that such power existed, and
Judge Richardson was of a like opinion. The
latter while assistant secretary had furnished
Senator Conkling of New York with a paper set-
ting forth, in clear and cogent terms, the argument in favor of the power, under date of 21
January, 1873.*

The President, naturally sympathetic and
warm-hearted, was inclined at first to grant what
was besought of him by those whom he had
been taught to regard as sound and far-seeing in
matters of finance. At that particular time the
President was taking a vacation at Long Branch,
not far from New York city. The Secretary of
the Treasury had remained at his post in Washington. Meanwhile as the news of successive
failures came over the wires, the excitement increased in volume, and more and more urgent
grew the appeal for help from the public funds.

The Secretary knew well enough that even if
he had an undisputed power to issue at once the

---

* A financial journal in New York city, that gave Secretary Richardson advice as to the management of the Treasury, spoke of him as "the
expositor of inflation."

entire reserve, it would be only adding fuel to
the flames, while crippling the Department, and
bringing it to actual repudiation; since a halt
would have to be called after a while in paying
the indebtedness of the government, as soon as
the reserve should have been exhausted. The
debts coming in for payment would inevitably
exceed the revenue to be depended on for meeting the public obligations.

We may pause here for a moment to view the
condition of the national finances as respects the
means at hand to sustain the public credit.

When Secretary Richardson came into office
(March, 1873,) the reserve of forty-four millions
in greenbacks had been drawn upon to the extent
of two millions, or more. The first thing he did
was to "take in sail and strengthen the reserve." *
By so doing, he had succeeded at the time the
panic came upon the country in accumulating
about fifteen millions of dollars.

The situation abroad with reference to United
States securities should also be borne in mind.

---

* The reason for this precaution lay in the condition of our imports.
For some years they had exceeded the value of our exports by several
millions of dollars. Plainly the country was getting into debt, and to all
debtors there must come a time of settlement and payment or a failure.
One or the other, so reasoned the Secretary, is always inevitable. When
the bureau of statistics had completed their tables for the year ending 30
June, 1873, Judge Richardson took the figures to President Grant and
pointed out to him the impending danger. He explained to the President
the plan upon which he was acting in order to strengthen the Treasury
by accumulations of money. As to this the President and Secretary were
in entire accord.

The Department, as we know, had a force of clerks in London engaged in carrying on the business of buying and selling bonds. Had it been telegraphed to London that the Treasury, unable to meet the ordinary obligations of the government, had stopped payment, there would have been a panic in London in United States bonds and the credit of the government would have suffered. It was due to the prudent management of the Secretary of the Treasury that there was not the least sign of excitement in London, and that our bonds maintained their former price, the credit of the government being in no wise impaired.

It seems that the pressure was great on both sides of the question of issuing the reserve. On one side, the administration was beset not to issue any more greenbacks, and to stop payment if necessary. On the other side, there were frantic calls for the President and Secretary of the Treasury to put forth the whole reserve. Both of these demands, Secretary Richardson resisted, and was sustained therein by the President, though (it must be added) not without great efforts and much argument on the part of the Secretary of the Treasury.*

---

* The following incident illustrates the courage of Secretary Richardson, and the good sense of General Grant. Upon one occasion the President telegraphed the Secretary from Long Branch to issue a large quantity of the reserve, and buy bonds and give notes the next morning, he himself starting for Washington that night. On arriving the next morning the President found that his Secretary had not obeyed the order. Going at

On Saturday, 20 September, the President telegraphed to Secretary Richardson from Long Branch, to meet him the next morning in New York city at the Fifth Avenue Hotel. The Secretary himself, at the office of the telegraph company in Washington, on Friday night at half past eleven o'clock, had written and sent a telegram to the sub-treasurer at New York, authorizing him to purchase $10,000,000 of bonds on Saturday. Arriving in New York early Sunday morning, the Secretary drove to the Fifth Avenue Hotel. Before taking breakfast, he went to the President's room and spent an hour with him, going over the situation, and pointing out the position of the department.

He took the ground that the Treasury must be kept strong for the sake of its own credit, and so as to be able to afford relief to the country after the panic was over; that a decision must be had at what amount to limit the bond purchase; that, with the concurrence of the President, he would limit the amount to $12,000,000, and stop there. Should all the banks suspend by agreement, then

once to the White House, the Secretary explained the necessity of keeping the Treasury strong and out of the whirlpool. A few words sufficed to explain why the order had not been obeyed. The President expressed his entire satisfaction that the Secretary had acted as he did.

Indeed, it may be said here that throughout his term of office Secretary Richardson enjoyed the fullest confidence of the President, who did nothing contrary to his advice. President Grant once said to Secretary Morrill, who at a later date had taken the Treasury, that he (the President) had never made a mistake when he had followed the advice of Secretary Richardson.

he would at once stop purchasing. He assured the President that it was their duty at all hazards to keep the department out of the panic. He pointed out the condition of affairs in London, and the effect upon our bonds should it become known there that the department was in any way unable to meet its obligations by reason of having expended its store of ready money. The reader must know that in 1873, the prospect of an ultimate payment of the national debt was not at all what it now is. There were very many persons, both in the United States and in Europe, who believed that in the end our bonds would not be paid. These and similar perils the Secretary pointed out to the President, who quickly grasped the situation.

Arrangements had been made for the interview with the President on the part of the bankers and business men. Ten o'clock was fixed upon as the hour. They had come to the hotel in great numbers. It was Sunday, but the hotel was crowded, and so were the streets in the neighborhood. A prominent republican senator, one of the foremost statesmen of the country, was there, as a guest of the hotel, and to judge from competent testimony he was the most frightened man on the premises. He seemed to be bewildered, and really knew not what to do.

Reverdy Johnson was also present, consulted

by the bankers, whom he furnished with a legal
opinion, taking the curious ground that under
the law, the President and Secretary had no
power to issue the greenbacks, but that if he
were in the President's place, he would feel it his
duty to issue them; and that in his opinion the
country would sustain the President in so doing.*

At the appointed hour, the President and the
Secretary took their seats at a table in one of the
large parlors, and the bankers, with others, came
in. Among those present were Commodore Van-
derbilt, Henry Clews, the Seligmans, George P.
Opdycke, Isaac H. Bailey, William Orton of the
Western Union Telegraph Company, William L.
Scott, Robert Lenox Kennedy, H. B. Claflin and
Mr. Vail, of the Bank of Commerce.

The excitement ran high. Many speeches were

---

* "The President without doubt is without legal power to issue any
portion of the forty million reserve. He says as much as that himself;
and on meeting me in the corridor asked my opinion about it. I told
him there was no legal warranty, but if I were in his place and deemed
that the exigency demanded such a measure, I would surely order it.
This has become a national calamity. To-morrow, unless relief is given,
all the city banks will suspend. The result would be a general suspen-
sion throughout the country, and a prostration unequalled even by the
catastrophe of 1857. The President coincided with me, and I am to write
him a letter on this subject at five o'clock." *Reported interview with Reverdy Johnson—New York Tribune, 22 September, 1873.*

It also appears that he advised that the sub-Treasury law had been
repealed, though it is not clear what use could be made of that fact. The
bankruptcy law had attached to it a schedule of repealed acts and amongst
them was the sub-Treasury act as well as other important acts. This was
a mistake clearly arising from an intention to repeal some parts of that
act, and had always so been regarded. *From a memorandum of Chief Justice Richardson.*

made, some of them almost violent in tone, calling upon the President at once to issue the whole forty-four millions reserve. The speakers said if the panic were not stopped, we should see the worst mob in New York the next day that had ever been known in that city; that already the streets were full of men, and in the morning the situation would be worse.

It seemed to have occurred to no one to point out how the reserve could be issued, or to designate the manner in which it could be put into circulation. The President sat perfectly calm. At last he said that anything to be submitted to him must be in writing, so that he could know exactly what they thought should be done.

The result of the interview was that a committee was formed, who retired for deliberation. An hour or two later, they had agreed to request that the Treasury Department would lend $20,000,000 to the banks, upon the receipt of clearing-house certificates, with a promise of more money, if necessary. This proposition was submitted in a writing, signed by firms and individuals, representing a large amount of money.

As affording an insight into the purposes of this historic interview, it may be helpful to append the text of this application to President Grant. It bore date "New York, September 21st, 1872," and read as follows:

The undersigned do respectfully represent to the President that, in the present situation of affairs, a financial deadlock will inevitably occur to-morrow unless relief be afforded by the government.

They respectfully suggest that no measure of relief will be adequate that does not place at the service of the city banks, twenty millions in greenbacks.

They respectfully petition the President to authorize the Assistant Treasurer to receive from the city banks, clearing house certificates, secured by ample collaterals and for which certificates all the city banks are jointly and severally responsible, and to issue to the banks in exchange therefor, greenbacks to the extent if necessary of twenty millions on such terms as to issue and redemption as may be satisfactory to the Secretary of the Treasury.

The undersigned deprecate any intention of soliciting a violation of the law. They believe that the above measure of relief is in strict accordance with the spirit of existing statutes and they are quite satisfied that it is indispensable to avert a crisis which would wreck the country to its centre.

The undersigned are firmly persuaded that this action on the part of the government would restore confidence immediately.

II. B. CLAFLIN & Co.	PEAKE, OPDYCKE & Co.
ANTHONY & HALL.	FRED BUTTERFIELD & Co.
HOYT, SPRAGUE & Co.	P. VAN VOLKENBURGH & Co.
WHITTEMORE, PEET, POST & Co.	J. M. BUNDY, "Evening Mail.",
PAYNE, GOODWIN & Co.	WM. L. SCOTT, Prest. 2 Nat.,
GEO. CECIL & Co., Logansport,	Erie, Pa.
Indiana.	GOODWIN & Co.
D. & A. KINGSLAND & SUTTON.	A. BOODY, Prest.

GEO. W. PERKINS, Cashier.

HARPER & BROS., Franklin Square.   S. L. B.

Fifty additional firms of the highest standing in the mercantile community were here and agreed to sign this paper, but so much delay was made in preparation that they have dispersed. Petitions have been sent to them to sign and ten thousand names can easily be obtained for signature.

Of course, as every one now perceives, there could have been but one reply given to such a request. The President could act only within the law; and there was absolutely no law that by any stretch of construction could be held to have converted the Treasury Department into a loan institution.* Such was the answer.

Several years after this occurrence the chief justice wrote out, somewhat hurriedly, a few notes of what had taken place, meaning to revise them at his leisure; but that leisure seems never to have arrived. These notes have been freely used by the present writer. What follows, however, is ex-Secretary Richardson's own language. The incident related has never before been made pub-

---

* Secretary Fish, writing from his country place, Garrison's, Putnam County, New York, under date of 22 September, 1873, to Secretary Richardson, says:

"I congratulate you, for I believe that the decision of Sunday will prove a step in the resumption of specie payments, which, I think, should be the object and the great financial feature of General Grant's second term, as the reduction of the debt was of the first. * * * I hope that it may be your lot to accomplish the restoration in value of the promises of the government with gold. You have a nation's thanks."

Writing to him again, on the 26th of the same month, Mr. Fish remarks:

" * * * I assure you that nothing that the President has ever done seems to give more satisfaction than the decision which you and he reached on Sunday last. I hear from everyone, except those interested in speculative stocks or bonds, one universal approval of the 'heroic action of the President and Secretary of the Treasury,' and but one expression of hope that you will adhere to the policy of non-expansion. It may be a severe remedy, but severe cases require severe remedies. * * * I agree with Henry Wilson in urging you to stand like a rock.

"Hoping to see you on Tuesday and in the meantime ready to do what I can to aid and sustain your act, I am, very faithfully yours."

lic; and it therefore seems allowable to print the roughly drafted outline as it stands.

Before their departure, the leading speakers had urged that the President and Secretary should go into Wall street the next morning, and be at the office of the Sub-Treasury, ready to do whatever was necessary. They stated that we should find the street crowded and the excitement intense. To this the President at once assented, without much consideration, but desiring to do all that was possible for the unfortunate men who were involved in the impending ruin. We had agreed to dine that evening at the Union Club where a large number of gentlemen were to be assembled.

When the room was cleared, I locked the door to keep out intruders, and with President Grant all alone, I said to him, substantially:

"Mr. President, the first thing now for us to determine is where we shall be to-morrow."

"Oh," said he, "I agreed that we would be at the Sub-Treasury in Wall street to-morrow to take such action as might seem necessary."

To this I replied—"That is just the place where we ought not to be, according to my view. The District of Columbia is made by the Constitution the seat of government, and the statute provides that all offices attached to the seat of government shall be exercised in the District of Columbia. In times of local excitement there is the place for public officers to be, away from the influence of frenzied people, and out of the reach of the mob.

"This panic was not brought on by anything done by the officers of the government, and nothing they can do will stop it. The merchants and business men of New York have caused the whole trouble; they have speculated, got overwhelmingly in debt, and are in deep water to which there is no bottom for them. The banks have all been encouraging them in their wild career and the bubble has burst. The banks have gotten them into this difficulty, for without the banks they could not have borrowed much money, and the banks alone can furnish the only relief to be attained. This is a case for action on the part of the banks and must be left to them to take care of.

"All we can do is to preserve the credit of the government by keeping its finances out of the panic. This can be justified before the people, and no other course ever can be. Besides, while the country everywhere is affected somewhat by this panic, there is no excitement except here in New York. The people of the West and elsewhere are calm and collected, and are looking to this city for every kind of demonstration. If there is to be a mob, here it will be, and the President and Secretary of the Treasury should be as far away from it as possible.

" What will the people outside of New York think and say if it be reported in newspapers to-morrow that the President and Secretary of the Treasury are in the midst of the mob in Wall street, at the Sub-Treasury, watching and awaiting results.

"Moreover, just as long as these men look to the United States Treasury for help, just so long they will do nothing to help themselves. They will hope and expect the Treasury to do everything for them, and it can do nothing whatever. The very fact of your being in Wall street will attract the crowd, and add to the chances of a mob ; and the rest of the country will behold with amazement that the President and Secretary of the Treasury, have left Washington and have, as they will think, joined hands with the money power of Wall street, of which the people are all jealous.

" My opinion is that our place in a condition like this is in Washington, aloof from excitement and where we can take a broader and cooler view of the situation. That is the place which the wise framers of the Constitution intended should be the quiet abiding place of public officers in times of local troubles; and if the public find we are *there*, they will feel great confidence and entire safety in the situation. If we are on Wall street, they will be filled with apprehension and fear at what may happen. In my opinion we ought to go to Washington to-night and keep away from Wall street and this excitement."

The President was convinced and agreed at once to my suggestion.

I unlocked the door, the President called Babcock (his private secretary) and told him the change in program that we had agreed upon, but charged him not to tell of it until after the great dinner that evening. Finally it was arranged that Babcock should have carriages at the Union Club house, and the President and I should slip out from the dinner separately, so as not to be observed and go directly to Washington. This plan was carried out, and the next morning we were at our posts at the seat of government.

Before the morning papers went to press our movements were known, and our whereabouts was announced in the first edition, and all New York knew in the early morning where we were. The result was that there was no further excitement, Wall street was as quiet as Sunday and no crowds filled the streets anywhere. The *Tribune* announced in large letters, "The panic over," and President Grant returned to Long Branch.

No intelligent student of our political history will now be found to question the wisdom of the Secretary's advice. Of the good sense exhibited by General Grant it may be said that it is precisely what would have been expected of him in the circumstances.

The firm stand taken by the President and his Secretary worked an immediate result. The banks, finding that the government declined to identify itself with the panic, and resort to strange and unheard of measures in an effort to restore confidence, took the only practical course open to them. They issued clearing-house certificates, and so contributed largely to allay excitement, and bring around again a normal state of the money market. While the panic was not entirely over, for it was temporarily renewed, the Treasury Department kept at its legitimate business and bought such bonds as were offered—the only lawful method of taking money from its vaults and putting it into circulation.

On 24 September, the Secretary at Washington telegraphed to the President at Long Branch as follows :

> If the panic continues unabated to-day, we must decide at what amount to limit bond purchases. The Treasury must be kept strong for the sake of its own credit, and to afford relief to the country after the panic is over. If you concur, I would limit the amount to about twelve millions and stop there ; and if all the banks suspend by agreement, I would stop at once. I don't think it is well to undertake to furnish from the Treasury all the money that frenzied people may call for.

As might be expected, President Grant approved of this sensible view; and Secretary Richardson pursued calmly his accustomed path, and thus "kept the Treasury Department out of the panic."

The requests, amounting almost to importunities upon the Secretary, to do something out of the usual course, with a view to relieving the strain upon the money market, were however kept up, notwithstanding the plain language of the reply already given. The president of the New York Produce Exchange, under date 30 September, 1873, urged a plan divided into two heads : *First*, that currency be immediately issued to banks or bankers upon satisfactory evidence that gold had been placed upon special deposit in the Bank of England in London, upon the credit of their correspondent there, to be used wholly for the purchase of bills of exchange. *Second*, that the President of the United States and the Secretary of the Treasury are respectfully requested to order the immediate prepayment of the outstanding loan of the United States, due January 1, 1874.

That such a proposition as the first request should be considered possible to be entertained by the President seems at this length of time strange indeed. A prompt answer was returned that to embark in such a scheme would involve the government in the business of importing and speculating in gold. It was entirely out of the question ; nor was it possible under the law to comply with the second request.

Through all these trying hours the President, in a manner most creditable to him, upheld the hands of his Secretary of the Treasury. The country was fortunate in having these two men at the head of affairs, for had a mis-step been taken it is fearful to contemplate how disastrous a wreck would have been made of the credit of the government. As it was, the firm conduct of the administration added a chapter to our public financial history that can always be regarded with a just pride by the American people.

The annual report to Congress of the Secretary of the Treasury 1 December, 1873, is a business-like document, that bears the impress of having been written by a practical man of affairs. Each important topic in turn is treated with good sense, the facts clearly stated, and the course of administration set forth in concise terms. Let any one to-day read this state paper with deliberation and he will be forward to acknowledge that the author approves himself equal to the discharge of the great trust committed to his keeping. There are exhibited here a broad and comprehensive grasp of public questions, sound reasoning and a conception of duty adequate to the situation. The report when critically examined distinctly enhances Secretary Richardson's reputation.

While he was assistant secretary, it may be noted that Judge Richardson, busy as he was, found time to prepare and publish a book of special value to all persons interested in a business way in the public loan. It was entitled "Practical Information concerning the Public

Debt of the United States, with the National Banking Laws for Banks, Bankers, Brokers, Bank Directors and Investors." Though professing to be nothing else than a compendium of the statutes upon the subject, it really contained not a little original matter in elucidation of the law. The volume made a timely appearance. Its chief excellence consisted in the arrangement of the various provisions of the statute law, and the means afforded, including an index, for speedy reference. It was designed to be a "handy book." Possibly its use by bankers in Europe was not left out of contemplation, the subject then (1872) being of extraordinary interest abroad as well as at home. A second edition of this useful publication was issued in 1873, when the author had become Secretary of the Treasury.

During his term of office at the head of the Treasury, Secretary Richardson received a flattering offer to become a member of a great banking house in London. The offer, though tempting from a pecuniary point of view, he did not care to accept. An opportunity presenting itself, however, for his going upon the bench of a United States Court for life, he resigned the office of Secretary and was made a judge of the Court of Claims. His name for the new position went to the Senate on the same day with that of Benjamin H. Bristow, of Kentucky, as his successor in the Treasury. Both nominations were speedily confirmed by the Senate, 4 June, 1874.

The Court of Claims, as its name indicates, is a tribunal in which claims against the United States may be submitted to the decision of judges. It was established by the act of Congress of 25 February, 1855, which provided for the appointment of three judges, to hold their offices during good behavior.* The jurisdiction of the court is confined to alleged obligations growing out of contracts. It does not deal with torts, except where Congress by special act refers a matter such, for example, as a collision in which a public vessel is charged as having been in fault, to the determination of the court.

The United States admits its liability to be sued, and prescribes how this shall be done. The Court of Claims has no jury, the court being judges of the fact as well as of law. As originally designed, the tribunal amounted to little more than a special committee of Congress; for it was the duty of the court to report to Congress, at the commencement of each session, and at the commencement of each month of the session, all cases upon which they had finally acted, together

---

* Judge Richardson contributed to the March, 1882, number of the *Southern Law Review* an interesting article describing the origin and growth of the court. This he expanded three years afterward into a pamphlet, entitled "History, Jurisdiction and Practice of the Court of Claims," a valuable piece of work, the source of much that the writer here presents, in relation to the subject.

with the material facts and their opinion, with the reasons of the opinion. The court also was required to prepare a bill in cases which received their favorable decision.

These requirements were the cause of so many delays that Congress later radically changed the organic act creating the court. By statute, 3 March, 1863, two judges were added, and an appeal given to the Supreme Court of the United States. The judgments of the court were to be paid out of any appropriation made for the payment of private claims. This desirable change had the effect to add to the importance of the court; and since that period it has dealt with a volume of business that year by year exhibits a steady increase.

At the time Judge Richardson took his seat upon the bench, Charles D. Drake, of Missouri, was chief justice; and Edward G. Loring, of Massachusetts, Ebenezer Peck, of Illinois, and Charles C. Nott,* of New York, were the other members of the court.

---

* During Richardson's occupancy of this bench his associates other than those named in the text have been J. C. Bancroft Davis, of New York (Harvard, 1840), 1877-1881 and 1882-1883; William H. Hunt, of Louisiana, 1878-1881; Glenni W. Schofield, of Pennsylvania, 1881-1891; Lawrence Weldon, of Illinois, 1883—; John Davis, of the District of Columbia, 1885—; Stanton J. Peelle, 1892—.

Upon the death of Chief Justice Richardson, Judge Nott was nominated and confirmed as chief justice of the court. The vacancy thus created in the number of judges was filled by the appointment of the Honorable Charles B. Howry, of Mississippi.

The court sat in rooms at the Capitol. In 1879, the space thus occupied being needed by Congress, the court was provided with larger and more convenient rooms in the building known as the Department of Justice, opposite to the north front of the Treasury, where it has ever since held its sessions.

From time to time Congress has committed to this tribunal certain subjects of controversy other than those falling within the strict language of the original act. One branch of jurisdiction, for example, involving a great many cases, and devolving an immense amount of labor upon the judges, is that of the French Spoliation Claims. The bar of the court is composed for the most part of lawyers resident at Washington; but cases of importance bring from time to time prominent lawyers of other cities before the court as of counsel for claimants.

A special assistant attorney general is charged with the duty of defending the United States in suits prosecuted in the Court of Claims. This official has assistants to aid him, who are also law officers of the government. While many cases involve questions of fact only, and others bring forward points of law of no general interest, it may be remarked that a great majority of the contested cases present features that are highly interesting, both in respect of the facts and the principles of law involved. Occasionally, a law question of very great importance comes on for argument.

A judge of this court, therefore, is not infrequently called upon to exercise the best powers of his mind in solving legal problems. While its business in the main lacks somewhat of that variety in subject matter and principles of law which abounds in common law courts, it yet embraces subjects of inquiry that are calculated to improve and strengthen the mind of the judges who deal with them. Sometimes a test case arises of novel impression, that is not only difficult of determination, but is highly important as governing the disposition of very large sums of money.

The new judge had reached fifty-two years of age when he took a seat upon the bench, destined to be for twenty-two years the scene of his continuous labor, and of his most pronounced intellectual triumphs. Here was his true sphere of action. If there can ever be an instance where a man of conceded ability and of unlimited capacity for work has found at last, after a varied experience, the one station exactly suited alike to his powers and his taste, surely the elevation of Judge Richardson to the bench of the Court of Claims furnishes that instance. The judicial gift that was his by nature he had made the most of in early manhood—and his strength undoubtedly lay in achievements of that character. With a mind developed by a course of training in national executive duties, rich in practical results, not least of which is to be reckoned the widening influence of foreign travel, he now returned to the field illumined by "the gladsome light of jurisprudence." It was an accession that obviously strengthened the court.

To be sure the present tribunal differed altogether from that in which he had gained his Massachusetts experience; but the points of difference were very largely comprehended in a knowledge of the practical workings and traditions of that great department of the government of which he had made himself so complete a master. The new judge went diligently to work. With what facility and exactness he performed the duties of the position may be seen upon consulting the opinions of the court, delivered by him and printed in the reports, from the tenth to the thirty-fifth volume, inclusive.

Engaged in congenial labors and blest with continued good health, the judge's prospect for the future was bright and unclouded. The sessions of the court were such as to permit a long absence from Washington during the summer vacation. Early in the season of 1875 the judge with Mrs. Richardson and their daughter started to make a tour around the world. When President

Grant learned of the project he signified his attachment to his friend by sending him a letter of introduction, under his own hand, to our officials abroad, commending Judge Richardson and his family to their kind attentions. The journey was a delightful one. The party went through Japan, into China, returning by way of Saigon (in Cochin China), Singapore, Ceylon, Aden, the Red Sea, and so through the Suez Canal and Egypt, and thence to more familiar points in Europe. The Judge hurried home to take up his duties at the court, leaving his wife and daughter at Paris, to pass the winter.

Late in the year Mrs. Richardson was taken ill with what developed later into an incurable disease. She was tenderly cared for by her daughter, yet in spite of all that the best medical skill and nursing could do the malady proved fatal. Mrs. Richardson died at Paris, 26 March, 1876. The young daughter bore up bravely, and alone made the voyage home with the remains of her dear mother.

The force of the blow to the devoted husband may not be a subject of estimation here. One might almost pronounce it a cruel thing that she should have been taken away at a time when he could not reach her bedside for even a last look of recognition. The chapter of their union in happiness unalloyed was closed. The lonely survivor turned to his studies and to his daily labor for

companionship; while the daughter took her place at the head of the household. Not long afterward Miss Richardson became the wife of Doctor Magruder of the Navy, and the young couple lived with the Judge. To provide for their comfort, quite as much as for his own, he built a commodious house at the northeast corner of H and Seventeenth streets,—where he lived (and the Magruders with him) to the end of his life.

In addition to his other occupations he accepted a professorship in the Law School of Georgetown College in 1879, and delivered law lectures there regularly until his resignation in the summer of 1894, when the faculty of that institution by unanimous vote elected him emeritus professor. In announcing to him their action, under date of 28 June, 1894, the faculty express their very deep and grateful sense of his "most valuable services as professor, extending over so long a period of years, almost indeed from the very inception of the school." The chair that he filled was that of statutory law and legal maxims. He was greatly liked by the students, for his lectures were practical, and delivered in a style capable of being readily understood.

Between the months of April and September, 1878, Judge Richardson expended his spare moments in one of those incidental occupations of which he was so fond. With an industry that is truly marvelous, considering the nature of his other engagements, he prepared in this interval, for the second edition of the Revised Statutes of the United States, a complete index that took the shape of two hundred and thirty pages, closely printed in double columns. This engrossing labor he was willing to enter upon for reasons disclosed only since his death, which are interesting to the public and highly creditable to the two men chiefly concerned.

His life-long friend, Governor Boutwell, it seems, had been appointed, under an act of Congress, 2 March, 1877, a commissioner to prepare and publish a new edition of the first volume of the Revised Statutes, the first edition not having proved satisfactory. When the Governor had completed his labors, and had in hand the manuscript ready for the printer, Congress passed a supplementary act, approved 19 April, 1878, requiring the commissioner to revise and perfect the index to the new edition. This formidable task, so entirely distinct from the duties of an editor, the distinguished commissioner shrank from undertaking. He knew, however, that Judge Richardson could perform this work if any man could, and he accordingly betook himself to his friend for help.

The Judge has left on record a statement of the circumstances in which he found it his duty to come forward and take upon himself the burden of this great responsibility. He says:

> Governor Boutwell came to me and said that he had never done such work and did not feel like undertaking it, and rather than do so he would resign, and would resign unless I would assist him. I told him that I would not assist, because an Index must generally be the work of one mind; that two men could not cut wood at the same time with one axe. The result was that he said I must make the Index and I agreed to do it.
>
> And I did make it, myself,—wrote out in manuscript every word and figure in the Index to the Second Edition of the Revised Statutes of the United States. Boutwell wanted to state the fact in his preface, but I objected to his mentioning my name. However he does make a nameless allusion to the fact. How well the work was done it must itself tell.
>
> To make it well required a thorough knowledge of the statutes themselves, which I had, for I had for several years annotated my own copy. The trouble with the first Index was that the maker used unimportant words found in the text, or words which did not convey the whole idea—the substance, without regard to the subject matter. I adopted a different plan. I used words which expressed the meaning and sense of the section, whether they were used in the text of the Revision or not; as, for instance, under "Auditors" I included the Commissioner of the General Land Office, and under "Comptrollers" I included the Sixth Auditor (Comptroller for the Post Office) and the Commissioner of Customs (who is auditor only and nothing else, for the customs business, and should have been designated as Third Comptroller). And so on through the whole Index, I was governed by meaning rather than by words. Governor Boutwell read the proof with me.

Of the execution of the work it is enough to say that the index remains a model of its kind.

At the earliest moment when it was permitted to the survivor to break silence, he took occasion to make the facts public and gratefully accord to his departed friend the credit due to protracted and unselfish labor. After commending the plan adopted by Judge Richardson, and explaining to what extent his handiwork applied, Governor Boutwell feelingly adds, "The death of Judge Richardson gives me the only opportunity that was possible of placing the honor of the index, which must mean something with the profession, to the credit of his name and memory.*

For a period of nearly eleven years Judge Richardson did his duty faithfully as a judge of the Court of Claims. Upon the retirement of Chief Justice Drake (who had reached his seventy-fourth year) President Arthur sent to the Senate the names of William A. Richardson to be chief

---

* Appendix, *post*, p. xlviii.

All the more praise is due to Judge Richardson for this achievement, because he was perfectly well aware how little is the gain to a man's reputation from the faithful performance of work like this. Indeed, he has said of index-making that, "most persons would not regard it as exhibiting a high order of merit." A man who is an index-maker and nothing else may be said to aim low, even though he succeed in making an admirable piece of work. Where such labor is performed, however, out of friendship, at intervals of time that by other men is made a period of leisure, its successful results awaken a grateful sense of obligation, no less than unstinted admiration for the unselfish motive that accompanies it. In view of the superiority of Judge Richardson's work, and the pleasing circumstances in which it was executed, his modest unwillingness, as now revealed, to be known as its author, affords us a phase of his character which his friends may justly admire.

justice of the Court of Claims, and John Davis
(then assistant secretary of state) to be a judge
of the court.* The nominations, which were
regarded with almost universal favor, were
promptly confirmed, 20 January, 1885. The
rules of the Senate were suspended that notice of
the confirmation of the chief justice might be
given immediately to the President and he was
sworn in the next day, 21 January.

Though the honor of a promotion had been
fairly earned, the new chief justice seems to have
determined by his administration of the office to
demonstrate that no mistake had been committed in entrusting added responsibilities to his
hands. He knew perfectly the opportunities of
the position, and he set about to improve them
to the utmost. In this praiseworthy endeavor he
met, it is no exaggeration to say, with complete
and enduring success.

In a presiding justice, personal qualities count
far more than in an associate member of a bench.
The chief justice is the executive of the court.

---

*The conjunction of the names of Drake and Davis serves to recall
the following slight incident: The writer had the pleasure of moving the
admission of Mr. John Davis, then a young lawyer, to the bar of the
Court of Claims. The court sat at that time in rooms at the Capitol.
Chief Justice Drake looked through his glasses, and said with a grim
smile: "John Davis! That is an honored name in this Capitol." The
allusion was to "Honest John Davis," once a Senator from Massachusetts,
the grandfather of his namesake,—the present accomplished and able
judge of the court.

Business feels his touch instantly. It lags, or it goes speedily forward, according as he is wanting, or is well equipped in the qualities needful for the control of affairs. The chief is the spokesman of the court; the official medium of communication between bench and bar. Much—one is tempted to say all—depends upon his manners and breeding. If considerate and courteous, it is well; if irritable and fussy, it is deplorably ill.

Lawyers who practiced in the Court of Claims were of one mind as to the qualifications of Judge Richardson to succeed to the post of chief justice. They united in saying that he proved himself everything that a presiding justice should be,— courteous, patient, ready to make due allowance for shortcomings of counsel, yet withal prompt, firm and insistent upon getting speedily to the real point at issue. He evinced a wonderful power of dispatching business. At the same time he displayed—and it is something more than tact—that nameless quality which encourages counsel to do their best, and yet can convey a suggestion— sometimes an urgent command even—without wounding the pride of the most sensitive recipient. You felt, while in his presence, that both court and counsel were working to their utmost, and yet there was no friction, no haste. The record of what the court accomplished during the eleven years or more that he presided over it, is to a measurable degree an honorable testimonial to his efficiency.*

A great deal of work is done by the Chief Justice of the Court of Claims in chambers. Of this it was justly said at the bar meeting held in his memory:

> The executive duties necessary to such a court, largely carried on in chambers and imperfectly appreciated by us as members of the bar, increasing with the years of the court, were enormous, but always met with a patience, a careful consideration, of which we have little conception.†

His thoughts were daily with the court. He studied to strengthen it and enlarge its sphere of action. One of his many vigils was to keep close watch upon Congress that they should take no untoward step in legislating with regard to a tribunal which they had created, the workings of which might readily be a subject of misconception. The enlarged jurisdiction of the court in later years is to be traced to him, yet he was scrupulous to guard against a radical change in its organization. In view of these and other like considerations, the reader may understand how engrossed

---

*A gentleman who had practiced before the court during the entire period that Judge Richardson was upon the bench says of him: "He was a splendid administrative officer. Nobody dispatched business so rapidly and so well. He was considerate of the comfort and convenience of the bar. If he saw a lawyer sitting within the bar, and he thought him to be waiting for the coming on of a case that he knew would not be reached, he would send down a note to him. This was his invariable custom. The bar all liked him."

† Appendix, p. xix.

was the active mind of the chief justice alike in the trial of causes, and in thoughts for the welfare, growth and permanence of the court itself.

It was a habit of the chief justice to bestow a good deal of care upon his opinions ; and as a result, besides being well reasoned, they are favorable specimens of a good judicial style. He rarely employed his pen in other fields than that of law; what little he accomplished beyond opinions and articles upon legal subjects, was chiefly confined to papers of an historical character.

As early as 1857 he was elected a resident member of the New England Historic Genealogical Society of Boston; and he was made an honorary member in 1873. In January of that year he was chosen an honorary vice-president of the society, and thereafter was elected annually to that office for a period of fifteen years. He had pursued investigations into the early history of his native town of Tyngsborough, and published a valuable article on that topic in the *Lowell Daily Courier* of 4 April, 1881. Upon one of his visits to England he made researches in aid of this local history, and he succeeded in bringing to light several interesting facts, that enabled him to correct errors in the statements of earlier writers. This modest undertaking was much to his taste. It is further to be observed that he contributed several articles to the New

England Historical and Genealogical Register of considerable importance.*

Proof sheets of one of these historical papers reached the house of the chief justice in Washington during his last illness, too late, however, to be submitted to his revision. The article in question was entitled, "The Government of Harvard College, Past and Present." It appeared in the January number of the *Register*, following his death. The same painstaking application appears here as in his earlier work. In order to prepare it he had consulted records, legislative and collegiate, covering a period from 1636 to the present day; and he has succeeded in producing an article which takes rank as authority upon a subject of which little has heretofore been accurately known. In a letter which he had sent with the manuscript to the editor, he observes :

The length of the article is entirely out of proportion to the time I have devoted to it. To condense a mass of matter which I have had to examine, into a short readable article on the salient points of the subject, has cost me much trouble and research.

I am the last survivor of those who were members of the board of overseers by the election of both the legislature and the graduates of the college. Of those who were members in 1863, when I was first elected, there are but two others still living.

---

* See bibliographical note in Appendix, *post*, pp. lxxvi, lxxvii.

The society of which he had been an honored member was not unmindful of the worth of such labor as his in the chosen field of early New England annals. The language of the following extract from resolutions adopted upon learning of his death denotes, it may confidently be believed, something beyond the ordinary expression of regret upon like occasions:

His interest in the future of the society was constant and generous. During his long connection with the society he was a frequent contributor to the pages of the Register. The death of Chief Justice Richardson is a public national loss, and this society, as only an inadequate expression of its regard for his services in behalf of accurate historical knowledge and good learning, adopts the following resolutions:

Resolved, That this society is deeply impressed with the value of the work and influence of Chief Justice Richardson in behalf of the objects for which it was formed.

Resolved, That his death is a special loss to the society and to historical students in general.*

Fortunately for the chief justice he had inherited an unusually good constitution. All his life he had been a temperate man and regular in his habits. As a reward, his health was for the most part vigorous, giving promise of length of years; but there can be no doubt that he put to a severe strain his power of endurance, by taxing himself with laborious application day after day.

---

* Proceedings of New England Historic Genealogical Society, upon the death of the Honorable William Adams Richardson (1897).

Not content to labor through the hours usually allotted to that purpose, he borrowed of time needed for sleep. He rose very early in the morning and went immediately to work. A large part of what was done by him upon the statutes he accomplished before breakfast.

His daily morning appearance at the consultation room of the court was an example of punctuality. Here he busied himself with scarcely a pause, unless when actually compelled by the presence of some one to turn away from the routine work in hand. During his period of three and twenty years upon the bench in the Court of Claims he never once missed a day in his attendance upon the sessions of the court, with the single exception of a week's confinement at home owing to an injury to his hand—a really remarkable instance of devotion to duty.

To even the mildest form of mental diversion he remained a complete stranger. Unlike most men, he cared nothing whatever for light reading, or for amusements such as billiards or a game of cards. It appears as though he had estimated the precise amount of time that he could devote to his chosen work, and that in so doing, he had purposely left no room for those moments of repose and recreation so needful in the daily routine of life.

His exercise was chiefly walking. He did not

take the vacations that others allowed themselves. Several times he went abroad in the summer (in 1893 he had crossed the Atlantic nineteen times); but upon these trips he was not idle; and his brain frequently was not permitted to rest while away from the desk. One might almost say that he had sat as judge at a trial of himself, had convicted the prisoner, and had sentenced himself to hard labor for life.

That such an unceasing stretch of work violated the laws of health can not be denied; and the chief justice sooner or later had to pay the penalty. When he had reached the allotted term of three score and ten, there was, it is true, no perceptible diminution of vigor in his walk and bearing. "He is one of those genial, sunny men," some one had earlier written of him, "upon whom time makes no impression." But not long after passing that milestone slight signs indicated that his many years were beginning to tell upon him. Still, he was constant in attendance upon his duties, and as ready apparently to go forward with the regular burden as ever.

In the summer of 1896, his friends were not blind to an admonition that his strength was somewhat abating. About a year before while in England he had a stroke of paralysis, from which he recovered by the best of nursing, so as to return home and resume his place upon the

bench. The fact of this warning was not generally known, but those close to him held it constantly in mind and could not but be aware that
his days of continuous labor were numbered.
The end, however, came more swiftly than they
had counted upon.

It so happened that the court had taken its
usual adjournment in the summer to meet on
the morning of Monday, 19 October. There is a
certain melancholy interest in noting that on the
very morning appointed for the court to assemble
for the new term, the chief justice passed away.
He died at his residence in Washington, on H
street northwest, at the northeast corner of 18th
street, about nine o'clock on the morning of that
Monday. He had been ill for about two weeks;
and yet, until shortly before his death, no apprehension had been entertained of a fatal result.

His daughter, Mrs. Magruder, her husband,
and their two children were living with him
at the time of his illness, and were present to witness how peaceful was the end.* The funeral
services were simple, as he would have wished.
They took place at All Souls' (Unitarian) church,
on the afternoon of Wednesday, 21 October. The
pallbearers were J. C. Bancroft Davis, Lawrence
Weldon, John Davis, Stanton J. Peelle, Frank W.

---

* Mrs. Magruder, his only child, did not long survive him. She died
at Washington, 4 April, 1898.

Hackett, George A. King, William A. Maury and Joseph J. McCammon.

The Reverend E. Bradford Leavitt, who but shortly before had been settled as minister to this church, conducted the services. His brief remarks were in perfect keeping with the occasion. He spoke of the long continuance in high public position of him whose body they were about to commit to the grave; and dwelt upon his tolerance and his faithfulness as a member of the church. The body was taken to the beautiful cemetery of Oak Hill (Georgetown), Washington, and laid beside that of his wife. "Man goeth forth to his work and to his labour until the evening."

A meeting of the bar of the Court of Claims was held in the courtroom on the forenoon of Friday, 20 November, 1896. Few lawyers of those accustomed to practice before the court were absent. A spontaneity and genuineness of feeling, that could not be misunderstood, pervaded the proceedings. The resolutions of the meeting, together with the remarks of those who paid their tribute of respect by speaking of the late chief justice, were far more interesting and impressive than is usual at such times.

The same is true of the occasion when the court received the report of the resolutions of the bar on Monday, 23 November. The Honorable Charles C. Nott presided, and there sat with the judges the Honorable J. C. Bancroft Davis, formerly a judge of the Court of Claims, and the Honorable Martin F. Morris, associate justice of the Court of Appeals of the District of Columbia. Mr. Justice Morris, besides being an intimate friend, had for many years been associated with the chief justice as a professor in the law school of Georgetown University. Mr. Assistant Attorney General Joshua E. Dodge offered the resolutions to the court in a few words happily expressed. He was followed by Mr. George S. Boutwell, who by vote of the bar meeting had been requested to second the resolutions. Allusion is elsewhere made in these pages to certain features of Governor Boutwell's tribute. Aside from the faithful portraiture that it affords, this brief address is worthy of special commendation for its undoubted literary merit. The Honorable Lawrence Weldon responded on behalf of the court. A single sentence will indicate with what discernment Judge Weldon had studied the mental characteristics of his chief.

He was highly educated in the perfect discipline of his mind, being enabled because of such discipline to bestow upon any subject of investigation the undivided and prolonged thought of his whole being; and that in the end is the perfection of education.

The event, one of the most important in the history of the court, was particularly grateful to the friends of Chief Justice Richardson and to the bar.*

The senior judge became chief justice; a new judge took his seat upon the bench, and the business of the court went on. But there were those about the court room,—judge, clerk, bailiff or faithful messenger alike,—who missed the figure and the kindly greetings of one who for well-nigh a quarter of a century had found here his happiness in daily toil. The traditions of the bar, already settling down upon the name and memory of the late chief justice, will deal gently with his faults, and speak in no uncertain tone of his diligence and his unswerving fidelity to duty.

---

*At a meeting of the Harvard Club of Washington resolutions were passed, speaking in fitting terms of the loss of one of its most distinguished members. The chief justice, with all his ardent love for the College, could seldom be prevailed upon to attend the annual dinner of the Harvard Club. He did come once or twice when the club was young and struggling, but his aversion to large dinners was enough to keep him away regularly, notwithstanding the fact that he remained in hearty sympathy with the purposes of the organization.

The graduates of Dartmouth College at Washington had a warm regard for Chief Justice Richardson, an adopted son, (for he received the honorary degree of LL.D. from that institution in 1886) as is shown by the following extract from the record of the proceedings at the annual meeting of the Alumni Association, held at the Raleigh on the evening of 19 January, 1897. On motion of S. R. Bond, Esquire, this resolution was unanimously adopted :

"In all the positions which he held he was distinguished for indefatigable industry, high conception of duty and incorruptible integrity, and the result of his labors will remain of lasting service to his fellowmen.

"It is appropriate that at this first meeting of the association since his death, in consideration of his affiliation with our *alma mater*, we should commemorate his distinguished life and services, and recognize the loss sustained in his decease."

HAVING THUS hastily surveyed the leading features of the ever busy life of the subject of our sketch, let us for a moment contemplate such traits of character as appear chiefly to have guided his conduct, and for the most part to account for the measure of success or failure justly to be accorded him.

These pages, it must be confessed, are fairly open to the criticism that stress has again and again been laid upon the fact that Chief Justice Richardson loved work. An intense love of work, however,—and it is not a hasty conclusion to say so,—is really the key-note to his character. He was to the last degree utilitarian. Born on a rugged soil, where generations had gained a subsistence only by the exercise of an indomitable energy, young Richardson from the first came under an inspiration to dedicate himself to toil in any direction where he could see that his labor would produce a good result. His mind was eminently practical. He had no idea whatever of what it is to "dwell in a world apart." He found himself in this working-day world at a very busy season, among people tireless and inventive; and his thoughts became engrossed in the hard-headed New England business of earning a competence, and making himself meanwhile of use and value to the community around him. Such were his aspirations.

Keeping in sight the predominating, not to say absorbing, influence of this idea of life's duty, let us examine what Judge Richardson accomplished respectively as lawyer, statesman and judge; and ascertain, if we may, what rank should be accorded to him among his fellows.

When a career has ended, we ask, was it a success? Though men differ widely in their estimate of what standard should be applied as the one true measure of success, yet they generally admit the life of him to have been successful in a certain sense, who, judged by the standard fixed by himself, has fairly attained the ends for which he has striven.

Judge Richardson started to make his own way in life with a plentiful stock of "common sense." He saw things as they were, and indulged in no vagaries. He meant to be a lawyer, as his father had been before him; and he studied hard to fit himself for the profession. He was a singularly modest man; in fact, had his nature been a little more aggressive, he doubtless would have impressed a sense of his real abilities more deeply upon those with whom he mingled. This modesty of his, amounting in some circumstances almost to timidity, probably accounts for the fact that he took no part in the contests of the bar,

where ready, off-hand speaking was required.
His preference, as we have seen, was from the
first for office practice.

He has himself well expressed the estimate in
which in his opinion a talent for public speaking
or forensic oratory should be held. That he was
content to yield to others the glow of triumphant
encounter at the bar, and felt it to be no great
deprivation, is apparent from the following language of an address delivered by him in 1869
to the students of the Columbian Law School,
Washington:

It is a mistaken notion, too often believed by young men,
that to be a lawyer, one must be an advocate, and therefore to
become successful after leaving the law schools one must be
an eloquent speaker. It is true that a mere advocate may
easily make a pecuniary fortune and gain extensive notoriety,
but if he is not something more his abilities thrive but for a
day, and he leaves little or no mark behind him. When his
contemporaries, who are charmed by his voice and manner
pass away, he is forgotten.

The real lawyer need not be an advocate, but he must be
a man of great acquirements and learning. He must be
learned in facts as well as in law. A lawyer in large practice
has more to do with facts than with law, and therefore the
more extensive his acquirements in all things which influence
the conduct of men, and affect the material interest of the
world, in the history of the past and in the passing events
of the present, the more certain and great will be his success.

He mastered legal principles after close study;
and since he gained his knowledge only by
long-continued application, he held it tenaciously,

and was always prepared to apply it to a case in hand. He may be said to have been a good lawyer, who had in him many of the elements that go to make up the great lawyer. It is safe to assert that no man in his day had acquired a wider or more thorough knowledge of the statute law than Chief Justice Richardson. From his experience in this branch of learning he came to possess great aptitude in construing the language of enactments so as best to express the legislative will. He also grew to be an expert draftsman, whose precision and accuracy could always be depended upon.

The following practical hints in dealing with the subject of drafting or revising statute law attest the truth of this statement. They are set forth in a paper drawn up by him and entitled "Some suggestions for revising the statutes formed after long and extensive experience and observation":

1. Never use the two words "the said" together. Either one is sufficient.

2. Avoid too frequent use of "any." The same idea may be often better expressed by "a" or "an."

3. In statutes relating to crimes and offenses, instead of the formula, "If any person shall falsely make," etc., say "Whoever falsely makes," etc.; or, instead of "Any person who shall steal," etc., say "Whoever steals," etc.

4. Instead of "*It shall be the duty* of the Commissioner of Pensions" (or other officer), etc., say "The Commissioner of Pensions *shall*" (Rev. Stat. U. S., secs. 3203, 4701, 4769, 4786,

etc.). Instead of "The Secretary of the Interior" (or other officer) "is authorized," etc., say "The Secretary of the Interior" (or other officer) "*may*." (Examples Rev. Stat. U. S., secs. 4776, 4777, 4778, 4780, 1704, etc.) The Revised Statutes abound in such expressions.

5. Employ no *provisos*, but divide each long section into two or more. (Rev. Stat. U. S., sec. 3173.) (It is difficult to use *provisos* with technical accuracy.) So with long sections without *provisos*. (Rev. Stat. U. S., secs. 639, 641, 643.)

6. Sections embracing the same general idea with shades of variations should be consolidated and rewritten. It is often easier to interpret one section than to construe several harmoniously together. (See Rev. Stat. U. S., secs. 1763, 1765, 1766, which have given rise to much litigation.)

7. There are many superfluous and worse than useless words in every section, which should be omitted or the section recast in more concise language.

8. Paragraphing is of great advantage wherever there are changes in the ideas, or divisions of the subject. (See striking example of the want of it in "The Compiled Statutes of the District of Columbia, 1894," "Descent," sec. 1, pp. 192, 193.) For example of its use see Supplement to Rev. Stat. everywhere. Cases cited should be in columns and not run together as in Rev. Stat. U. S., margin of secs. 629, 639, 649, 652.

9. Material changes in the language should be explained in notes, pointing out the object and whether or not any change in the law is intended.

10. Most of these suggestions are just as applicable to drafting new acts as to revising old ones, and in all law documents, such as deeds, findings of fact, and opinions, may be observed with advantage.

Judge Richardson's career upon the bench of the Court of Probate and Insolvency of his native state has already been characterized as eminently successful. He there dealt with a range of subjects in which he had made himself second to no man, for thorough acquaintance with the law. The systematic and orderly procedure of the court, even the regularity with which numerous details are rapidly taken up and disposed of, were to him specially pleasing. In what to many minds seemed a maze of complications and perplexities, he saw only an opportunity for deducing order and perspicuous arrangement. Though the work in time got to be largely a matter of routine, the Judge enjoyed it; and one reason why he enjoyed it may have been because it was left for him to explain to both lawyers and laymen the real simplicity of a system, otherwise by them indifferently well understood.

Of course the thought occurs to the reader that there must inevitably be some risk of a lack of breadth in a life entirely spent in work such as this; but a timely transfer to the new and untried duties of an assistant secretary of the Treasury, rescued Judge Richardson from any such consequences.

A man whose native bent is judicial, and who has enjoyed the experience of many years' training upon the bench will, if suddenly transplanted to an executive life, rarely make a success of the new undertaking. This is eminently true of a judge whose predominating tastes are those of the student, rather than those of a practical man of affairs. Judges are aided by argument from counsel, and they deal with questions that they have time carefully to consider. The bench to a large extent follows precedent. Its chief business is to ascertain what legal principles rule the facts, as settled by the evidence. There are times, to be sure, but they occur rarely, when a supreme test is made of the courage and fearlessness of the court, whether a single judge, or consisting of several judges sitting in bank. The ordinary experience of men in judicial position, however, is not of a character to foster readiness to incur responsibility.

As has already been intimated, the subject of this sketch had in his makeup not quite enough of that bold, aggressive and self-confident spirit, which one to be a successful leader of men must possess. It is indeed a rare quality. Natural disposition, early training and long continuance upon the bench had fitted Judge Richardson rather for the quiet contemplation of the merits of a legal controversy, than for rendering off-hand decisions of what ought to be done in this or that urgency involving large responsibilities.

When Judge Richardson came to Washington it was to enter a field of public duty altogether different from that to which he had been accustomed. It was an interesting work, however, and although for three years he continued to regard

his absence from Cambridge as a temporary one, he soon began to adapt himself to the new conditions. At this post, as we have seen, he did faithful service, and achieved what his friends deemed a gratifying measure of success.

Later, upon being advanced to a higher office, where all the responsibility rested upon his own shoulders, he had to meet requirements immeasurably graver. A host of questions, many of them of momentous consequence, demanded instant decision. He was brought face to face with many perplexities, some of them growing out of the action of men in high political station, who sought to impress their views upon him, or have him grant their personal requests. Secretary Richardson, it must be observed, had not served in the State legislature or in Congress; and his actual experience of the ins and outs of political life was necessarily limited.

It would do this honest and pure-minded public servant a great injustice to assert that he lacked the nerve to refuse point-blank a political request; or that he betrayed too ready a disposition to yield to strong and persistent pressure. Such is not the fact. But in the many emergencies requiring the quick exercise of an inflexible will, and the daring to go ahead, be the consequence what it might,—he felt a need which a sterner and bolder nature would not perhaps have recognized. Ex-Secretary Boutwell, his life-long friend, who knew better than any one else the strong and the weak points exhibited by Judge Richardson in his administration of the Treasury, alludes to this phase of his character, as follows:

I have once made this remark in a public way: There is a rough side to government, and there must be a quality of harshness in those who administer governments successfully. Such generalizations, even if true as rules of action, are subject to exceptions. If it had been the fortune of Judge Richardson to have served on the executive side of the government for a period of years, and there had been any just cause for criticism, it would have had its origin in the absence of the quality of harshness in his nature.*

In advancing this statement the writer must not be understood as intimating that Secretary Richardson lacked anything of courage or ability in the prompt decision of large questions of state, such, for example, as are laid before his cabinet officers by the President in the general administration of the government. Here it is indisputably the fact that Secretary Richardson manifested a clear insight, and a praiseworthy readiness to assume the fullest measure of responsibility. It was rather in matters of importance ranking above merely minor questions of administrative routine that he was disposed to refer to precedent, and look to the views of others around him—a course very natural for one whose training had hitherto been almost exclusively judicial.

---

* Appendix, pp. xlvi, xlvii, *post.*

There is of course a vast amount of routine work going on at the Treasury of which the Secretary from the nature of things can know but little, no one man having time or strength to give it personal supervision. But the head of that great department, like the general in command of an army, makes himself felt, so to speak, all along the line. The traditions of the department are to the effect that in Secretary Richardson's day energy was infused into the channels of ordinary business, and subordinates worked cheerfully under the eye of their chief. He was popular throughout the department.

Public questions of great magnitude, as has just been remarked, were sure of receiving at his hands prompt and wise disposal. The Secretary relied upon his own unaided powers wherever necessary. His cool and courageous action during the panic of 1873 richly entitles him to grateful remembrance as a resourceful and trustworthy officer of the government. Indeed, his reputation may be safely left to the record of service rendered in that trying emergency. It is speaking within bounds to say of Secretary Richardson that in his official acts his motives were pure, his diligence unwearied and his judgment uniformly sound. To an eminent degree faithful in his great trust, he secured the affectionate esteem of General Grant, and gained the respect of all who were closely connected with him in administering the affairs of the government.

Says ex-Attorney-General George H. Williams, the only surviving member of the cabinet of which Secretary Richardson was a member :

I was favorably impressed with his executive abilities as the assistant of Secretary Boutwell, and used my influence with the President to secure his appointment as Mr. Boutwell's successor. Judge Richardson never said or did anything to produce a sensation. His ambition was to perform his public duties faithfully and honestly, without ostentation or display. He was modest and unassuming, and in my judgment was not current in popular estimation at his real worth. He has left an enviable reputation.*

Mention has already been made of the conspicuous fitness of Judge Richardson for a seat upon the bench of the Court of Claims. There were able lawyers on that bench during his incumbency, but no one surpassed him in the possession of those qualities which are specially needful to command the highest measure of judicial success. He was greatly respected and liked by the entire bar.

It had seemed to the writer, therefore, peculiarly appropriate that the testimony of the bar and court to the true position held by their deceased brother should be preserved in the form of an appendix to this fragmentary sketch, in order that the reader may resort to these authoritative

* MS. letter, Portland, Oregon, 19 July, 1897.

sources, and learn with what measure of respect men who knew him intimately agree in estimating his talents and acquirements. It were unfitting to attempt to add anything to what is there said with so much acuteness of observation —so much precision and integrity of expression. For no one can lend ear to the utterances of that occasion, and fail to be struck with their sincerity of tone and their wholesome freedom from exaggeration. They are words of honest praise. To a degree rare in like circumstances, the portrait of the man is outlined with striking fidelity to the form and feature of the original. It is much to have deserved such a tribute; yet those who knew the chief justice from the vantage ground of intimate acquaintance will say that his memory does in truth deserve it—every word.

We may in a spirit of hearty approval borrow the language of one of the most discriminating of the speakers, who thus felicitously sums up the leading characteristics that in his opinion entitle the late chief justice to be classed among the most eminent of American jurists:

Thus reviewing his judicial attainments, I think that without danger of undeserved eulogy we may say that the minute accuracy of his knowledge, his capacity for hard work, his quick apprehension of the issue of a case, his sound judgment and his convincing expression of his conclusions, entitle him to rank among the great lawyers of the nation.*

---

* Mr. William B. King, Appendix, page xxxiii, *post.*

That Mr. Richardson of the Middlesex bar developed into a model judge of probate, and later became an excellent judge of a federal court, —rose to be its chief justice and administered that responsible office with unparallelled skill and ability, is not to be wondered at when we reflect that it was the strict rule of his life that when upon the bench he should never attempt to be anything else than a judge. His aim was single. It was with a far-seeing design that he had limited to himself the scope of his exertions. Within those self-imposed limits we may plainly see his to have been indeed a

Life of endless toil and endeavor.

All his days he was a student of law. Aside from something of current political measures, he appears to have cared for little in the world around him except the tribunal in which he sat, and its steady growth and development in the public favor. He concentrated all his powers upon the judicial office. A will of iron confined his efforts to that circle within which it was his ambition to excel. Broad and general culture is an almost necessary equipment for a judge; and the chief justice did not shut his eyes to the fact, but the test he first applied to a subject was, is it immediately useful?

Such a course of conduct as this, pursued year after year, by a man of native ability, could hardly fail of its object; and it made of William Adams Richardson, if nothing else, a superb master of all the varied duties of his office. So complete a dedication of self to the accomplishment of one supreme end is rarely witnessed, except in the lives of men who possess elements of greatness. His triumph, for it was a triumph, came as the reward of sheer grit and perseverance.

As might be expected, his time was engrossed in the study of legal questions, leaving little opportunity for the enjoyment of general literature, or the fine arts.* The habit of persistent industry in the line of his chosen occupation so grew upon him that he found his happiness only there. What he called relaxation took the shape of labor given to the compilation of statutes, or by way of indexing, or other like employment, of a nature not far removed from the severer duties of the judicial office. He would, for example, be up at early day-light, working on the statutes, and deem it a species of leisure entertainment.

This capacity and liking for work in one direction is reflected in his writings — most of which are opinions announcing a decision of the court. While his style is clearness itself, a certain precision void of any attempt at ornament

---

* It could not be truthfully said of him, as it was of his class-mate Sprague, that " He breathed the still air of delightful studies " ; except that it was an incomparable delight to Richardson to study the intricacies of the statutes.

or illustration reminds us that the writer is rather intent upon reaching a conclusion by a sound logical process, than to attract or enlighten the reader. There are no allusions that indicate an acquaintance with the great writers; no lingering fondness for the classics; no glimpse of a world of fancy beyond that in which men carry on traffic, and disagree as to their rights.

Let it not be inferred from what is here said that the subject of our remarks was uncompanionable. On the contrary, though he eschewed general society and the club, he was of kindly disposition, most considerate of others, tactful and responsive to the friendship of his intimates, and the courtesies of every-day fellowship. Indeed, there were few men with whom it was a greater pleasure to converse. He spoke only of subjects that he knew something about, and he was ready to listen attentively to those who were perhaps better informed than he. A good talker, of animated manner and pleasing voice, he never committed the mistake of being disputatious, or of displaying a readiness to monopolize the conversation.

One of his strong points was a tenacious memory, and those who were privileged to hear him talk of the judges and lawyers of the earlier day knew with what relish he could tell an anecdote, or illustrate a phase of character. He had schooled himself to be accurate, and he liked to have others accurate in what they said. Not infrequently he would allude to some prevailing error, in popular usage, and do his part towards correcting it. Himself methodical and orderly, he wanted to see others careful in these respects. What keenness of observation he possessed has already been alluded to; it seemed as if nothing could escape him.*

It was the misfortune of Chief Justice Richardson that he was not a man of a large and commanding presence. He was of medium height and size. In mixed company his manner was somewhat retiring and unobtrusive. Whether this was due to innate modesty, or was the result of an acquired liking for the contemplation of the study, one may not easily divine. But

---

*Take, for instance, the court and bar: he used to note any peculiarity in those who practiced before him. He said of a certain member of the bar that he had a habit of bringing a book down violently upon the table, making a great noise. Another gentleman had a peculiarity of gesture that was annoying. Said the chief justice, "He is a young man of talent, and sometimes I have thought I would speak to him about it. It is a sweep of one arm, very unpleasant and ungraceful to witness." "Another member of the bar," the judge continued, "has a habit of rising upon his toes when he is speaking, a practice by no means pleasing to the bench." So, of a writer's style: Upon one occasion somebody spoke of a lawyer who constantly used the word "practically." Another of the company remarked of a practitioner that he seldom went far in oral argument without employing the word "thereupon." Chief Justice Richardson said if the opinions of Chief Justice Bigelow of Massachusetts were examined it would be found that he was much given to bringing in the word "familiar." "Upon familiar principles" is a phrase frequently recurring with him. These are trivial illustrations of Chief Justice Richardson's habit of noticing slight peculiarities.

with all his acute power of observation, his tact and his knowledge of human nature, he was not disposed to mingle freely with others, or take a prominent part in the company in which he happened to be thrown. This trait may be considered unfortunate, because without doubt it contributed to a public estimation of his abilities and his talents that was below his deserts. Many a person may have been in his company for a brief season, and come away with an altogether inadequate impression of his real ability.

A fair conception of how the chief justice looked may be gained from the excellent engraving by Stuart, of Boston, that faces the title page. It is proper to add, however, that the photograph from which it is copied, being of early date, has not reproduced those lines of thought furrowing the brow which, in the recollection of those who knew him while he was chief justice, had imparted to his looks a perceptibly greater degree of intellectual force than is here portrayed. His was one of those countenances that light up and beam with animation, when not in repose. There was something cheery about him when you met him and spoke to him.*

He was a familiar figure for many years in the

---

* Of portraits there is one in the Treasury by Stagg (formerly of Boston) and a good piece of work by Robert Hinckley, of Washington. A less satisfactory work by an Italian artist hangs in the court room of the Court of Claims at Washington.

streets of Washington—on foot, for he preferred walking to riding.

In his family relations he was kind and affectionate—a most devoted father. To his grandchildren he was particularly attentive. He would himself buy their presents at Christmas and at other times, going to great pains to select articles that he knew would give them pleasure. His practical turn of mind is evinced by the fact that he left behind him a letter for his grandson, with instructions that the seal shall be broken, and the letter read by him, on reaching his one and twentieth birthday.

Of his friendships, it may, with truth, be said, that no man prized a friend more highly, or was more loyal in his attachments. The circumstance that his taste withdrew him largely from general society rendered him all the more sensible how precious was the possession of a true friend. Many of his more intimate associates he had outlived. The relation between him and his honored predecessor in the Treasury, continuing unbroken as it did for so many years, is beautifully illustrated by the spectacle of the survivor standing in the presence of his juniors and paying tribute in words of chastened eloquence to the memory of the departed.

The great statesman of England who this summer (1898) has been laid to rest enjoins it in his will that no laudatory inscription be placed over him. In a like spirit it would have been the wish of William Adams Richardson that the record of what he has accomplished, with no word of praise thereon, be left to speak for him. It may chance, however, that a solitary copy of these pages shall escape the ravages of time, and convey to some curious reader, years after all the actors of this period have long been asleep, some knowledge of the events recited here. If he would care to learn what form of words might best sum up the aspirations and the achievements of him in whose memory this brief story has been told, let him know the simple truth, "He was content to be useful."

APPENDIX

PROCEEDINGS OF THE BAR
AND OF THE COURT

· MEETING OF THE BAR.

A meeting of the Bar of the Court of Claims, called by a Committee of the Bar, was held in the court room, at eleven o'clock of the forenoon of Friday, 20th November, 1896. The attendance was unusually large. In calling the meeting to order Mr. Assistant Attorney-General Dodge, speaking for the Committee, said :

Upon so impressive an event as the death of the Chief Justice of the Court before which we practice, especially when that event, as now, breaks an association between counsel and judiciary extending through the larger part of a generation, it is meet and proper that we should pause in our struggles to testify to each other our memories of the one who has gone from among us, to note those qualities which have won from us confidence and affection.

We have among us one distinguished by an intimacy of association with the deceased, extraordinary in its character, an intimacy in professional life, in official life and in close personal friendship, which has extended through a period longer than the lives of most of us. It has seemed to the Committee, and it seems to me most eminently proper that I should ask that associate in profession, fellow in official life and warm personal friend of our Chief Justice, to preside over us. I therefore present to you the name of the Honorable George S. Boutwell to be the presiding officer of this meeting.

Mr. Boutwell, accordingly, was chosen to preside. On motion of Mr. John W. Douglass, Mr. Archibald Hopkins was elected Secretary.

Upon the motion of Mr. Maury the Chairman appointed the following gentlemen as a Committee to withdraw and report such action as might seem suitable : Messrs. William A. Maury, Joshua Eric Dodge, John W. Douglass, W. H. Robeson, George A. King, Frank W. Hackett and Alexander Porter Morse.

The Committee, after having retired for a brief season, returned, when Mr. Maury said :

Mr. Chairman, I am directed by the Committee to make the report which I hold in my hand, and which, with the permission of the meeting, I will now proceed to read :

The death of Chief Justice Richardson brings to mind Lord Coke's remark, adopted from Seneca, with reference to the death of Littleton, that "when a great, learned man (who is long in making) dieth, much learning dieth with him." So true is it that the parsimony which saves to earth the smallest atom of our dust has no place in the realm of the spiritual. It becomes, therefore, an office which we owe not only to the great dead, but to ourselves, to commemorate the qualities which made them great, that, at least, the remembrance of those qualities may not also perish from the world, and with it the incentive of great examples.

The late Chief Justice was one of the strong

influences which Massachusetts has contributed to the Union, and which have entered largely into the warp and woof of the National greatness.

Duty and usefulness were the twin stars that guided his career. Under their influence his painstaking, laborious diligence seemed to have no limit but that of his capacity of endurance. In whatever he undertook there was completeness of execution. His revision of the statutes of Massachusetts, and his supplemental revision of the statutes of the United States, earned him general commendation; and the same fidelity of performance marked his administration of the offices of Secretary and Assistant Secretary of the Treasury.

But it was in the Court of Claims that his greatest work was done. There he presided to the entire acceptance of the bar and the public, and, if possible, strengthened the hold of the Court on the general confidence.

The terseness, accuracy and thoroughness of his judgments proved his fitness for the judicial station, while his dispatch and administrative talent gave him admirable efficiency as Chief Justice. To sum up his character as judge, he never delayed justice to any, nor did he remove a single landmark of the law.

> *Resolved*, That the Bar of the Court of Claims deplore the death of Chief Justice Richardson as a serious loss to the National judicature; that they recognize in him an upright, able and

learned Magistrate, who contributed much to the establishment of justice in the land, and that they hold in grateful remembrance the courtesy and consideration he uniformly extended to them.

That the Chairman is hereby requested to furnish the Assistant Attorney-General in charge of the Government's business in the Court of Claims with a copy of these proceedings, with the request that he will present the same to the Court, and move that they be entered in its minutes.

That the Chairman is hereby requested to transmit a copy of these proceedings to the family of the deceased, with an expression of the sympathy of this meeting.

REMARKS OF MR. WILLIAM A. MAURY.

Mr. Chairman : Before submitting the motion, which I now make, for the adoption of the Report, I feel that I must allow myself the gratification of saying a few words, and then give way to other gentlemen who are more competent to speak of the late Chief Justice.

As one who had the honor of intimate relations with the Chief Justice, I can truly say that his death has left a wound which time will scarcely heal. You can bear me witness, Sir, that those relations, in which you participated also, taught the lesson of the value and the beauty of friendship with more effect than what Cicero and the other moralists together have written on the subject; the difference being between virtue in energy and virtue as an abstraction.

You also, Sir, have, in common with myself, felt the elevating and helpful effect of contemplating his even, tranquil nature, his long-suffering patience and perfect charity, his affectionate loyalty and sympathy, his refusal to harbor resentments, and his uniform disposition to overcome evil with good.

But now, Sir, "when anything lieth on the heart to oppress it," we shall look in vain for the *particeps curarum* to whom we have long been accustomed to turn, and shall miss the grasp of his vanished hand.

Need I say here, in the midst of all these witnesses, that the late Chief Justice possessed admirable qualities for the Bench? He was just, able, learned, laborious and prompt. He worked with facility, and with such energy and concentration, that formidable difficulties seemed to melt away before him.

But I must not omit to refer to another valuable distinguishing trait, that love of accuracy which was to be seen in everything he did. I was particularly struck with it about a year ago, when he was preparing an article, for some periodical, on the occasionally mooted question, whether the presiding judge of the Supreme Court should be styled "Chief Justice of the United States," or "Chief Justice of the Supreme Court of the United States." A somewhat similar question having, in late years, arisen in England, with regard to the proper title of the Lord Chief Justice there, his restless desire to get to the bottom of the subject and exhaust every possible source of information led him into correspondence with Lord Russell. Need I add, Sir, that, by the time he completed the article, nothing remained to be said that could be said on the subject? It was this habit of accuracy that prevented him from slurring over his work, and gave a satisfactory completeness to whatever he did, whether it was. great or small.

His experience as Secretary and Assistant Secretary of the Treasury was useful to him as a judge, rendering him the better qualified to add to the mass of valuable learning to be found in the Court of

Claims Reports, in connection with a large variety of questions affecting the administration of the Executive Department of the Government in its various branches.

The thoroughness of his supplemental revisions of the Statutes of the United States, and the marks they bear of painful labor and research, intensifies my regret that he did not accomplish a general revision of the whole body of the written law of the Federal Government.

During his last illness, his power of will supported him while he was completing the index of the current number of the second volume of his Supplemental Revision.

Too much can not be said in his praise for undertaking that laborious and exacting work when age, with its infirmities, had begun to tell upon him. The remuneration was small, a mere pittance, and the sole inducement that impelled him to put this new burden on his already bending shoulders was the unquenchable desire to be useful in every way he could.

I trust, Sir, that you, or some other competent hand, will be invited to prepare a sketch of the life and labors of the late Chief Justice, to accompany the next volume of the Supplemental Revision, when it shall be completed, that his fellow-countrymen may know how much they owe to this man of useful toil.

The last time I saw him, which was a very few days before his death, his countenance shone with an extraordinary brightness, I was going to say effulgence, which I had never observed before, and which I could not but think was the joyful expression of his pure soul as the hour of its release drew near. Thus we see with what cheerfulness the mortal puts on immortality who has the testimony of a good conscience and is in perfect peace with all the world.

Mr. Chairman, our dear friend has left an example which we may hope will "reach a hand far thro' all years" with its lesson of "nobly to do, nobly to die."

REMARKS OF MRS. BELVA A. LOCKWOOD.

Mr. Chairman : I feel it a duty imposed upon me to-day, to say that I cordially agree with the resolutions that have been presented, and that I heartily endorse the same. I have been a member of this Bar for seventeen years, and it seems very pertinent that I should add my testimony to the uniform courtesy, kindness, and to the justness, to the indefatigable work of the Chief Justice of this Court, who has always been accessible, always approachable, whether on the bench or in chambers. This has been particularly impressed upon my mind for the reason that I have recently been requested to testify to a prominent historian of Belgium and Germany, as to the treatment which women receive in this country from the Bench and Bar, and I then most cordially testified as to their uniform courtesy.

I most heartily give my testimony to the uniform kindness, to the fairness, and to the achievements of Chief Justice Richardson, the late deceased.

REMARKS OF MR. JOHN W. DOUGLASS.

My first acquaintance with the late Chief Justice was when he became the First Assistant Secretary of the Treasury under Mr. Boutwell. After he had succeeded to the Secretaryship, I saw him daily, as my position of Commissioner of Internal Revenue required constant consultation with the head of the Department.

He was affable and easy to approach on business, evidently being animated by the desire to do his duty promptly and with an eye single to the good of the public service.

If I mistake not, it was while he was Secretary that the radical change in the machinery of the Internal Revenue system was inaugurated, by which change some eleven or twelve hundred of the assessing officers were dispensed with, and the assessment of taxes transferred to the main office in the Department. This reform in the civil service, though it struck off a large number of the political friends of the administration in every State of the Union, had his hearty support, and the result justified his interest in the movement.

When I left the Treasury Department in the spring of 1874, and returned to professional occupation, the Judge was on this bench. Here, also, he was always courteous, attentive and patient ; and his labors were unremitting, as was his habit whenever and at whatever employed.

I met him once while he was engaged on the digest of the United States Statutes, and, in reply to my inquiry, how he found time enough outside of his judicial duties to perform the other work, he replied that the work on the statutes was largely done between daylight and breakfast time. While the large majority of us were in bed, he was probably up and busy with his additional labors. A life of well-put activity, as his was, is a blessing to the country that enjoys it, and a just pride and joy to associated friends.

On another occasion, a little while after the Bar meeting in honor of the late Chief Justice Drake, in conversation with Judge Richardson about that occasion, he said rather pathetically : " Well, Douglass, some of these days you will be at a meeting of the kind for me." I replied, "Whenever that happens, Judge, the speeches and resolutions will be such that your family and friends will rejoice in them." He smiled and we parted soon after.

He was a good and faithful servant from first to last, in every place that he held, and is now reaping no doubt the promised reward.

REMARKS OF MR. JOHN B. COTTON.

Mr. Chairman and Brethren : Interesting and instructive as it may be to review the earlier years of Chief Justice Richardson, during the long period in which he was judge of probate and insolvency in the great Commonwealth of Massachusetts, and in its most active and populous centre ; his part in revising and editing statutes ; duties which laid the foundation for similar work in a broader and national field, the fruits of which every counselor practicing in state or national tribunals enjoys ; his connection with that great executive department of the Government, the Treasury of the United States, where he imbibed a varied knowledge so essential to the right solution of intricate problems in this Court — it is as Justice and as Chief Justice of the Court of Claims that I knew him best, and in this sphere I shall speak of his connection with the Bench and Bar.

I hazard nothing in saying that, of the multitude of tribunals, from that of the most simple and limited jurisdiction in the State to that of the highest in the nation, there is none of which the more than seventy millions of our people have so little knowledge of the character, the scope of investigation, of the practice and decisions, as that of the Court of Claims.

Its growth for almost half a century has been pre-eminently an evolution. So silently has this development been that, notwithstanding the importance the Court has attained, outside a limited circle of practitioners its real value is either unknown or unappreciated. One of the distinctive features of our federal system is that it has relations, not with States, but with the citizen personally. Our English ancestry considered the King the "fountain of justice." The ordinary tribunals were insufficient to supply in many instances remedial justice, and an innate sense of right found expression in the petition to the sovereign.

That could hardly be called the most perfect form of government in whose constitution could not be found some germ whose unfolding would give the citizen a means of obtaining and enforcing rights of property and contract. This he has found in the Court of Claims. I am a firm believer that the time will come when, by a still further evolution, torts done a citizen by the Government will have a more certain source of remedy than the legislative branch of the Government.

This is not the occasion to trace the steps by which the Government has created this tribunal. Its history is portrayed in one of the last works of our late Chief Justice.

That Chief Justice Richardson appreciated the philosophy upon which the Court of Claims is founded is seen from his quotation of the words of that eminent lawyer, Charles O'Conor. "The Court itself," he says, "is the first born of a new judicial era. As a judicial tribunal, it is not only new in the instance, it is also new in principle. . . . Prior to the institution of this court, all rights as against the nation were imperfect in the legal sense of the term ; every duty of the nation was a duty of imperfect obligation. There was no judicial power capable of declaring either ; no private person possessed the means of enforcing the one or coercing the other. . . . But we are authorized to look higher than the mere convenience of suitors and the dispatch of public business. Enlightened patriotism will contemplate other and more important consequences. Caprice can no longer control. Here equity, morality, honor and good conscience must be practically applied to the determination of claims, and the actual authority of these principles over governmental action ascertained, declared and illustrated in permanent and abiding forms. As step by step, in successive decisions, you shall have ascertained the duties of Government towards the citizen, fixed their precise limits, upon sound principles, and armed the claimant with means of securing their enforcement, a code will grow up giving effect to many rights not heretofore practically acknowledged.''

Engrossed, brethren, in what we are pleased to term the practical duties of our profession, we are too apt to lose sight of the fact that we best honor it by ever keeping in view the equally high obligation of building to the ideal system.

Such was the judicial organization, then and still imperfectly reaching upward, to which William A. Richardson was called as a Justice in 1874, and of which he became Chief Justice eleven years later. His advent was in a most fortunate period of his life ; not too old to have lost ambition, not too young to fail to realize the importance of his position. The years during which in his native State he had presided in a court,—the creation of statute rather than of common law,—and yet requiring a knowledge of the common law for successful administration, were in some respects a preparation for a court whose vital breath is drawn from statutes, and yet so comprehensive in its jurisdiction that one unskilled in the learning and practice of the common law, can be neither a useful judge nor a successful practitioner.

Judge Richardson brought to the Court something quite as essential as the knowledge thus acquired; a practical knowledge of structure, traditions and practices of one of the great departments of the Government, as well as an acquaintance with those of all the others.

He brought a "faculty of nice discrimination," methodical arrangement, natural as well as acquired by his already long experience in the study and compilation of statutes. I am aware how easily, on an occasion like this, we can pass from the regions of cold criticism to those which are warmed by our affections. But I fully believe it would be difficult to conceive a mind better prepared for the duties of Judge of the Court of Claims than that possessed by William A. Richardson, on his advent to this Bench.

My personal recollection of Judge Richardson dates from the time I became an officer of this Court. But my knowledge of him is founded not alone on personal intercourse. It is gained from the spirit which pervades and gives tone to the decisions, the practice and traditions of the Court of Claims ; for it is old enough to have traditions. His influence is in all of them. From these sources I am able, to my own mind at least, to answer satisfactorily what, in part, ought to be said of the record of his life.

Predominant in Judge Richardson's life, was an intense devotion to the welfare and upbuilding of the Court projected to bring about those conditions which I have quoted from the eloquent words of Charles O'Conor. So earnest was this interest, that those who were fortunate enough to possess his confidence, knew that at times he was apprehensive that by some caprice the power that gave it birth would recall its life. The apprehension was sincere but unfounded. The Court of Claims may be enlarged to greater usefulness but not destroyed. These apprehensions can only be accounted for by his jealous devotion.

This devotion has been shown in other directions. Where in the history of courts can we point to a judge whose life was more exclusively given to a single object than was Judge Richardson's ? Rarely absent from his seat on the Bench, the few hours each week, which in common with his brethren he gave to the hearing of cases, formed but a small portion of the time occupied by him in its duties. Term time did not measure it. The long vacation hardly knew a cessation from his labors. His opinions rendered failed fully to evidence his work. The executive duties necessary to such a court, largely carried on in chambers, and imperfectly appreciated by us as members of the Bar, increasing with the years of the Court, were enormous, but always met with a patience, a careful consideration of which we have little conception. For more than twenty years Judge Richardson literally devoted his life to the work, denying himself the pleasures which others take, and when he did break away from its routine, he carried with him something to do which should, by way of information or otherwise, redound to the benefit of the Court.

Of the quality of his work, as embodied in his opinions, there can be but one mind. Our views of the work of a judge may be as much prejudiced by favorable as by adverse judgments. Every well-balanced mind will eventually settle itself aright, aided by time and reflection. That so few of Judge Richardson's opinions have been overruled by the Supreme Court, is a deserving tribute from that august body. He watched the results of review by that Court, not merely upon his own opinions, but those of all the members of his Court, and had a pardonable pride whenever its judgments were affirmed. When overruled I have on occasion heard him gracefully acquiesce in the justness of the decision. Judge Richardson in his written opinions did not always confine himself to a mere statement of the facts and law of the case. Designedly or otherwise, his mind seemed naturally to regard it as appropriate in many cases to give a full and complete history of a statute, or practice. The utility of such a course is undoubted. The earlier reports of many tribunals have been in some degree text-books for students of the law. That Judge Richardson's opinions frequently embody his varied and extensive knowledge of the history of the statutes and customs of the Government, is no slight addition to their worth.

How shall I speak of his relations with the Bar? On an occasion like this any past irritations between the Court and the Bar, happily few here, fall into merited oblivion. When it is remembered that the cases of individual attorneys, few compared with the aggregate number on the docket of the Court of Claims, probably exceed that of any court in the land, if not in the world, and that like an avalanche, these cases are poured down upon this Bench, one does not wonder that the late Chief Justice, who so well knew how valuable was time, should early in a hearing seize upon the vital points of the case and urge their consideration. Such suggestions were always kindly made, and no right-minded member of our Bar ever had cause to resent them. Sometimes suggestions were mirthful; they never had a malicious sting. He believed this a business Court. What he desired was a clear-cut statement of the law and facts relied on.

The Court of Claims is pre-eminently patient under lengthy discussions. Whatever might be his view of the utility of the argument, rarely did Chief Justice Richardson interfere to shorten it. Our minds are not always receptive in the excitement of an argument, and we often fail to see the force of the

Court's suggestion. Seldom in such a case did Judge Richardson persist. More often he allowed us to proceed according to our own notions. To be satisfied that we have had a fair hearing, is a large factor in ending litigation. Either designedly, or from intuition, Judge Richardson acknowledged the force of this idea.

He believed that no technicality should dispose of a case when possibly a fuller exposition of its merits would decide it otherwise. Until there was a complete exhaustion of its merits the Chief Justice was unwilling to close a cause. So he frequently pointed out to counsel the weakness of their position, and allowed them to strengthen it, if possible. It is questionable whether a closer observance of some of the technical rules of common law practice would not benefit the Court and parties litigant. But to this Judge Richardson was opposed in theory and practice. Hence his unvarying kindness to the members of the Bar in all the details of business.

I would not if I could disassociate my personal relations with the late Chief Justice from those which were once official. I want to give my tribute of grateful praise to him, when, coming into a new and untried field, I ever found him ready to explain the practices and theories of the Court, so different from those in which I had had experience, and made smooth many a path in an unknown field.

Others will speak of his varied learning on curious legal topics; of the facility with which he wrote of them, and of his relations outside the Court. But here I knew him best and of that I have spoken.

His days were lengthened by much doing. To state it as a little more than three score and ten would be unfair to his memory. We have seen him, brethren, in these latter days come into and go out of this room, battling with ill health, yet always assiduous in his duties, courteous and attentive. He has departed, not because there was no more work to do, but because the machinery, grown frail with years, could not longer perform its functions. Our restricted vision does not comprehend all he has wrought. That it has been much we know. How much, no one save Him whose eye is all-embracing can tell.

REMARKS OF MR. GEORGE A. KING.

My acquaintance with Chief Justice Richardson did not begin till he had been many years a member of the Court of Claims. Thus his judicial services to his native State, as also his career in the Treasury Department as Assistant Secretary, and later as Secretary, are to me but a part of the history of the country, except in so far as they were brought more prominently to my notice through the interesting personality of the Chief Justice, and his conversation about his past life while occupying these positions— a style of conversation which was of very frequent occurrence with him, as in later years he lived much in the past, and delighted to recall his busy, young life, both as a judge in Massachusetts and as a financier in one of the most critical periods of President Grant's administration.

During the greater part of the time of my acquaintance with him he was the presiding officer of the Court. In such a tribunal as the Court of Claims, where a personal appearance of either parties or witnesses is of the rarest occurrence, and where the proceedings are conducted wholly between counsel and the Court, and largely in writing, there is no very marked difference between the duties of the Chief Justice, and those of the other members of the

Court. Generally speaking, however, the Chief
Justice is both the presiding and the executive officer
of the Court As presiding officer, his personal
manners and bearing exercise a considerable influence over the general tone and temper of the tribunal,
and may render its atmosphere an agreeable one, or
otherwise, to the members of the Bar practicing
before it. In this particular, Chief Justice Richardson made his Court a decidedly pleasant one in which
to practice, especially for the younger or less experienced counsel who happened to come before it. His
manners were uniformly suave and affable, and he
was always ready to bear with patience the natural
timidity and nervousness of counsel addressing for
the first time a national tribunal whose jurisprudence
and practice occupy so different a field from that of
every other in the country, whether State or National,
as to render experience before other courts of compar-
atively slight value. At the same time, his remarkable quickness of apprehension made him impatient
of mere platitudes, and he was apt to insist with
some strictness, though it never could be called asper-
ity, upon arguments being addressed to the precise
point before the Court. His own judicial opinions
are marked by the same characteristic. They are
uniformly terse and direct and generally confined to
the precise point involved in a case. Where anything
outside of this is given, it is purely for purposes of
illustration or analogy. But few of his opinions can,
like many of those in the reports of the Supreme
Court, be read as complete essays upon any one
branch of the law. Sometimes, however, as in the

McKnight Case, in the 13th Volume of the Court of Claims Reports, he made an exception to this rule; and in that case the most complete statement of the system of Treasury accounting ever given is made the basis of his opinion; while, five years later, his opinion in the *Hodges* Case, in the 18th Court of Claims Reports, is a summary of the history of the Captured and Abandoned Property Act, and of the business done under it. These, however, are somewhat exceptional, and in the very few instances of this kind, it will be found that the digressions from the exact point involved were usually made for the purpose of putting on record historical facts which were not to be found in any standard treatises or other works on the subject. As more usual samples of his judicial method, I should name such opinions as that in the *Johnson* Case, in the 14th Volume, on the Doctrine of Presumption of Regularity of Official Acts; or the *Hitchcock* Case, in the 27th Volume, on the Assignment of Claims against the United States.

His turn of mind was eminently practical. For this reason he but rarely placed upon record a dissent from the opinion of the majority of the Court, even when he had not concurred in the decision. He regarded the decision when made by a competent majority, as the resolution of the Court, to be made the basis of action; and which it were better not to weaken by suggesting even well-founded doubts of its correctness.

His mark will long remain on the jurisprudence of the Court; and he took great and just pride in the prominent part he had taken in the evolution of the present system under which demands against the Government are to the utmost attainable extent taken out of the region of political or personal favoritism and are brought as completely within the domain of scientific jurisprudence as is the law of real property, or of patents.

In politics he was from earliest youth a staunch Whig, and an ardent Republican from the very inception of that party. The only perceptible influence of his political views upon his judicial opinions is in the broad and generous view which he always took of the powers of the General Government. There was certainly nothing sectional in the spirit of his decisions, which were as just to the war claim of the South, or the Indian depredation of the West, as to the French Spoliation claim of his native New England. He regarded all citizens as alike entitled to the protection of the General Government, and to the fulfillment of its obligations to them, in whatever part of the country they might live.

In religion he was during all his life a strict member of the Unitarian communion, and during his residence in Washington was an active participant in the work of All Souls' Church, of which he was trustee for three terms of three years each. He will be specially mourned by his fellow-members of that Church, where his regular attendance and hearty co-operation were for so many years a contribution to its welfare and advancement.

REMARKS OF MR. JOHN C. CHANEY.

Chief Justice Wm. A. Richardson was among my first acquaintances in Washington. He impressed me from the first as a man of even temper—a Judge who always wanted to be right. He was an indefatigable worker, a conscientious judicial executive officer. His education was supplemented with abundant energy so that the business before the Court went speedily on.

The members of the Bar of the Court all recognized his fairness in the methods and purposes of the Court. He was jealous of the dignity of the Court, which was a source of pride to the people of the United States. The judicial office holds such a relation to the affairs of men that its dignity is as sacred as the ermine with which the judge is clothed. The Court of Claims of the United States is one of the most important courts in all the land. The variety of questions constantly recurring, and the amounts involved in the cases brought in this court, make it a great tribunal in the economy of the Government. It is the people's court.

The dignity of the office held by Mr. Justice Richardson is second only to that of the Chief Justice of the Supreme Court of the United States. Judge Richardson appreciated this, and in his bearing on and off the bench there was never occasion for unfavorable criticism. He liked responsibility. He liked work.

Congress has for years looked to him for the compilation and revision of the statutes of the United States ; and the Revised Statutes bear the impress of his genius and his zeal for a convenient and ready reference to the modifications of the laws inherited by the country.

His learned associates all recognized his quick conception of the statute law. While in legal erudition he may have been surpassed by others who sat with him in counsel, he rarely ever erred in the application of the law to an established statement of fact.

My tribute to Justice Richardson is, that he was a man of wholesome integrity and candid sociability, a learned, industrious lawyer and a conscientious, upright judge. The Bench and Bar have not suffered by his administration of the Court's business.

Now that he has been so suddenly called to his reward, it will lead us all to a more kindly consideration of the labor imposed upon the Bench in its search for the truth, as revealed by the laws it is called upon to interpret.

I have an abiding faith in the immortality of the soul. I believe that this life is the nursery where the soul is prepared for transplanting in the great orchard of eternity, there to go on in growth, expanding and brightening—glorifying the Creator ; that if the ledger-book of life shall unfold more assets than liabilities, the world has been made better by that life ; that if a man has been faithful over a few things he shall be made ruler over many things.

Judge Richardson measured up to his responsibilities. The lessons of his life are useful to us, for in them is the inspiration of duty well done. The high position he attained is worthy of all praise and is the precious heritage of his family and friends.

REMARKS OF MR. WILLIAM B. KING.

The late Chief Justice Richardson said on more than one occasion that he considered the work done by him, which was of most value to his fellow-men, to be the revision of the Statutes of Massachusetts, undertaken over thirty years ago ; that this, in his judgment, outweighed his services on the bench of this Court. While this work, he said, had received no extraordinary amount of express commendation, he had felt that it had served its purpose well because almost no adverse criticisms had ever been heard upon it. He thought with that acumen which always distinguished his mature judgment, that the failure to find fault was a higher tribute to the merit of an impersonal work, such as the revision of statutes, than abundantly expressed praise. The correctness of this opinion is strikingly illustrated by the fact that more than three hundred errors in the Revised Statutes of the United States were found and corrected by statute within a few years of the revision, while many more have been pointed out but never corrected.

We who are familiar with the work of the late Chief Justice in this Court are not willing to accede to his estimate of its value as secondary to his earlier work, but would rather ascribe his opinion to the essential modesty of his character, leading him to depreciate the importance of the particular work in which he was at the time engaged.

The qualities first noticed by every observer as marking his work in this Court were his great learning in matters of administrative and statutory law, his knowledge of the details of every case, and his untiring industry. These were always first spoken of. Yet I think that these are among the lesser distinctions of his intellectual character. These qualities—industry, knowledge of details and specialized learning—must be possessed by every great lawyer; yet a lawyer may have them all and not be great. There are other qualities possessed by the late Chief Justice that constitute the essentials of a great legal mind, but his unassuming appearance and his modest manner failed to thrust upon those associated with him, so prominently as otherwise might have been, the fact that he had the highest qualities going to make up a great lawyer.

Foremost among these was his ability to discern the real point at issue in any case. This is the crucial test of either an advocate or a judge. A lawyer may study his cases for many days, he may saturate himself with erudition, he may master even the minutest details of a controversy, but unless he possesses that rare and unusual quality of separating the chaff from the grain, of throwing aside the husk and shell and reaching the kernel, of seeing clearly the real point of a case, all his labor is but gathering material for a greater mind to use. When we consider the swiftness with which Chief Justice Richardson seized the issue in every case, often before counsel had fully stated it; when we recall that he never allowed his mind to be diverted from it during

the trial ; when we remember the courteously con-
cealed impatience with which his mind received un-
necessarily prolonged explanations of unimportant
details, we realize that his industry and learning were
crowned by the possession of that quality which is
the first in constituting a great legal mind.

And if to see the point of a case is the first legal
gift, to express it so as to carry conviction to others
is only secondary. Here indeed he was no less able.

In older days, the charm of a writer was thought
to be the possession of some special, yet self-conscious,
style. But the literary canon of the future seems to
be that the best use of language is that which leaves
the reader unconscious of the writer and impressed
only with his thought. *Summa ars celare artem* has
taken the place of all other rules. It was this which
marked the writings of Chief Justice Richardson.
The first impression on reading one of his opinions
is intellectual conviction. The reasoning advances
by sure steps to a correct conclusion. A demonstration in mathematics is the most perfect expression of
logical reasoning, and I think that his opinions came
nearer to this form than is found in the opinions of
any but a few, and these the greatest, judges. In
reading them, the mind is kept intent only upon the
subject, unconscious of the writer or of the style. It
is only after they are carefully examined that one
realizes the exactness and conciseness of expression,
and the clearness of the reasoning process by which
the result is reached. The appearance of effort is
entirely lost, yet those familiar with the methods of
his work know that some of these opinions were held

under consideration and amendment for many successive months before reaching their final form.

United to these qualities was one of the most valuable in a judge, soundness of judgment, called in plain speech sometimes "common sense," because very uncommon. It is generally the result of the action of a broadly synthetic mind upon an intimate knowledge of all the facts relating to the subject. This led the late Chief Justice to avoid the merely technical side of every case and to see its substantial justice. Therefore, while his mind moved on strictly logical lines, it moved with a broad comprehension of the justice underlying each case and of the relation which the law declared in this particular case bore to the whole body of law on the subject. This breadth of vision prevented his judgment from being led astray by technicalities and gave it that soundness which is one of its chief characteristics.

Thus reviewing his judicial attainments, I think that without danger of undeserved eulogy we may say that the minute accuracy of his knowledge, his capacity for hard work, his quick apprehension of the issue of a case, his sound judgment and his convincing expression of his conclusions, entitle him to rank among the great lawyers of the nation. That his work was of a highly specialized kind, brought directly to the attention of but a small class of his fellow-citizens, prevented his great ability from receiving the wider recognition which it would have had in some other tribunal, perhaps of far less importance, but of greater publicity.

It is, therefore, mere justice to his memory that

we, who know his work and appreciate his ability, should here declare our estimate of his intellectual character.

His kindness to the younger men at the Bar is a matter which should not go unmentioned. It grew with his advancing years. No young and timid practitioner ever could complain of a rebuff. Youthful earnestness was always a safe-conduct to his consideration. Ability in a young man was constantly recognized. I have heard him more than once speak with appreciation of the efforts of the younger members of the Bar and express his hope for their success. Indeed, I should be wanting in due regard for his memory if I failed to declare my personal obligation to him for the repeated suggestions and sound advice which he has often given me as to the correct method of presenting cases in court.

With all the personal modesty which marked him, the Chief Justice had a high opinion of the dignity of this Court. One need only recall his opinion in the case of *Meigs*, reported in the 20th Volume of the Reports of the Court (p. 187), where the Treasury Department had refused to follow the judgment of this Court on a later demand of exactly the same nature by the same claimant. The opinion reviewed the laws and decisions governing the relations between this Court and the Executive Departments, with this conclusion :

> "Thus the course of legislation unmistakably indicates the intention of Congress that the decisions of the Court of Claims shall be guides and precedents for the executive depart-

ments in all like cases. The wisdom of such legislation and of the intention of Congress indicated thereby is manifest."

It was through his article on the "History, Jurisdiction and Practice of the Court of Claims" that more general public attention was invited to the Court and to the great importance of its jurisdiction. The eloquent words of Charles O'Conor, quoted in this article, and which have been referred to by a previous speaker, give a true picture of the work of the Court:

"Here equity, morality, honor and good conscience must be practically applied to the determination of claims, and the actual authority of these principles over governmental action, ascertained, declared and illustrated in permanent and abiding forms. As step by step, in successive decisions, you shall have ascertained the duties of government toward the citizens, fixed their precise limits upon sound principles, and armed the claimant with means of securing their enforcement, a code will grow up giving effect to many rights not heretofore practically acknowledged."

For twenty-two years the life of the late Chief Justice was devoted to this end, and he died at a time when the ripest fruit of his mind was in this form given to the benefit of his country. His fame may well rest upon his services to justice in this tribunal and a permanent result for good to his fellow men will be found in the inestimable aid rendered by him in the establishment of the law controlling the relations between the citizens of the United States and their government.

REMARKS OF MR. ASSISTANT ATTORNEY-GENERAL CHARLES B. HOWRY.

Mr. Chairman : We have met to commemorate the life, character and services of the late Chief Justice of the Court of Claims. Nothing we can say can soothe " the dull, cold ear of death," but the language of eulogy is the tribute which the living are wont to express to the memory of the useful and the good, and those who live and follow the custom of according to those gone before the proper meed of praise for their actions here below thus unconsciously render homage to public and private virtue, and the good which death has claimed in those of whom we speak.

It is fitting that the Bar should assemble to do honor to the memory of Judge Richardson, not only because of his usefulness as a man, but his excellence as a judge; and in assembling to honor him after his labors are over, we honor ourselves and the community and country he served so well.

Merely to have lived three-quarters of a century signifies but little. Length of days and many years come to many, and material existence to old age is accorded to millions. But to have lived more than three-score years and ten, to have occupied high and honorable position, and to have attained prominence in the pursuit of useful ends and purposes, and finally to have died with the respect and esteem of men, signifies much and quite enough to justify honor and praise from those who live.

Coming to this city three years ago, my acquaintance with Judge Richardson began at that time. Thus it may be said I came to know him in the evening of his days. Under these circumstances others can speak of his life work and to what he accomplished far better than I can, and I will not sketch his career. But official relations brought me in constant contact with him and with the Court over which he presided, and I came to know him not only as a judge, but as a man, and to appreciate his many acts of official wisdom and personal kindness. Where I had a right to expect only official respect and courtesy, evidences of personal regard were not long wanting in my relation with Judge Richardson which each recurring season strengthened to such an extent I felt that in him I had truly a friend. So many evidences of this good will on his part were given to me from time to time, I shall always esteem my relations with him as one of the most pleasant memories of my official relations with the Court, of which he was the presiding Judge.

We all know that men of strong individuality often possess some great distinguishing traits of character, which in life largely control their actions, and in death becomes manifest as still the ruling passion. Historians tell us that Augustus Cæsar died in a compliment and Tiberius in dissimulation, while the hand of God fell upon Vespasian in a jest. Judge Richardson died at his work. He was the incarnation of work. His eye was on everything connected with the Court and the work of the Court, and his vigilance over the details of every part of the business in hand was something extraordinary.

He had great pride in his work and always seemed solicitous to be right, not merely because his action could be reviewed, but from an earnest desire to reach just and proper conclusions. Reminding him upon one occasion of Lord Bacon's warning that judges ought to remember that their office is *jus dicere* and not *jus dare*, to interpret law and not to make it, or give law, else it would be like the authority claimed for the church, and that no torture could be worse than the torture of the laws, — he was quick to respond to my objections to judge-made law that he hoped his opinions would lead an impartial public to say that he had followed his office *jus dicere*.

The Chief Justice had great consideration for the time and convenience of others ; keen appreciation of the difficulties which beset those assuming the prosecution, or charged with the duty of defending cases. He was ever ready to smooth the asperities engendered by the heat of active practice and the conflicts of the Court room. He was obliging and courteous, impartial and just, attentive and vigilant, cautious and careful of the rights of litigants, and in his death the Court of which he was chief has lost an able coadjutor, the Bar a friend, and the country an upright, good and capable judge. I will not say more, because worthy ends and expectations were attained by the late Chief Justice, and many warm and close friends are here ready to speak to what he did and what he was, while the splendid fabric of judicial work wrought by his care and patience and earnest endeavor in quest of truth will stand longer than anything we can say.

On motion of Mr. Abrams the Resolutions were unanimously adopted by a rising vote.

The meeting also voted that when the Resolutions should be presented to the Court on Monday next, the Chairman of this meeting (Mr. Boutwell) be requested to second the same with such remarks as he may desire to make.

MR. BOUTWELL : The chair will accede to the wish of the members of the Bar and will second the Resolutions on Monday morning.

Thereupon, on motion of Mr. George A. King, the meeting adjourned.

PROCEEDINGS OF THE COURT.

Monday, November 23, 1896.

Present: The Hon. CHARLES C. NOTT,
                  LAWRENCE WELDON,
                  JOHN DAVIS,
                  STANTON J. PEELLE,
                                      Judges.
          J. C. BANCROFT DAVIS,
          Ex-Judge of the Court of Claims.
          MARTIN F. MORRIS,
          *Associate Justice of the Court of Appeals
          of the District of Columbia.*

Mr. Assistant Attorney-General JOSHUA ERIC DODGE addressed the Court as follows:

May it please the Court: At a meeting of the Bar of this Court held on Friday last, November 20th, said by some of the older members to have been the most representative and largely attended meeting held within their memory, there were delivered numerous addresses commemorative of the character and services of the lately deceased Chief Justice, William A. Richardson, which it is hoped will be compiled in print and given permanence, either as a part of a memoir of the life of their distinguished subject, or by incorporation into the next volume of the Reports of the decisions. Many of them were eloquent, and all were worthy of a place in the history of the Court which he so long adorned.

The meeting also directed me to present at this time the following resolutions, with a motion that they be spread upon the permanent records of the Court :

[Mr. Dodge, after having read the resolutions, continued.]

These resolutions were but the crystallization of the sentiments of bereavement, affection and admiration which pervaded that meeting of men, many of national rank and fame, who for many years had been in the contact of daily business affairs with the deceased. The sudden breaking of that routine forced upon each the realization that with all his modesty and unobtrusiveness, there had lived among us and gone from among us a man great in his generation.

With such realization comes almost perforce the query, ever renewed and always but imperfectly answered, What is greatness ; What qualities of mind and of heart constitute it ? None can answer by a generalization. We can but analyze the qualities of each individual, and sometimes satisfy ourselves what element of his character most led him to his measure of success in life. The man who has gone from among us commenced his life in an obscure little hamlet among the northern hills of Massachusetts, distinguished only by its name, Tyngsborough, which, as Chief Justice Richardson himself discovered, is not shared by any other community in the United States. Why did it not run its course and end there among the petty but respectable duties, pleasures and affairs which make up the lives of so many gentlemen of education and intelligence, instead of reaching out into the government and courts of his State and of his nation, so that when the end comes, the great places of his country are troubled, and those charged with cares and duties as broad as this great country are brought to pause therein and to note that one high among them is no more?

To me it seems that the great dominating force in this career is an eminently practical and useful one, and one which in large measure can be developed and cultivated by all, so that this life may stand out as a most useful guide to those who yet have in much portion their lives before them. A never-tiring, never-flagging devotion to the duties cast upon him, more than anything—perhaps more than all things else—distinguished our Chief Justice. Whether the duties were great or small, to them were devoted all of his excellent intellectual power, all of his ready tact and sound common sense, and all of his persistent industry ; and in the progress of his career from his hamlet home in Tyngsborough, through all the gradations to the nation's capital, and the control of some of the most important affairs of state, his life was a repeated fulfilment of the promise that "he who has been faithful over a few things shall be made ruler over many things."

Mr. GEORGE S. BOUTWELL said :

May it please the Court :

As a solemn duty I second the motion that has now been made that the resolutions which have been adopted by the Bar of the Court of Claims, in which the members have attempted to set forth their appreciation of the character and services of the late Chief Justice, be placed upon the records of the Court and made a part of the day's proceedings.

Before I speak of his services and standing as an executive officer and a jurist, I shall avail myself of the opportunity now presented, that I may recognize the early, long-continued and uninterrupted friendship that subsisted between the late Chief Justice and myself.

Our acquaintance began in the last half of the decennial period following the year 1830. At that time neither of us had attained to his majority. William Adams Richardson was a pupil in the Academy at Groton, Massachusetts, and I was a clerk in a village store. He entered Harvard College in 1839, and for several years our ways of life diverged. Our meetings were casual only, but our friendship continued, although in politics we differed until we came together in the Republican party. Upon his graduation from Harvard College in 1843, he began the systematic study of law in the city of Lowell, which became his residence for many years.

During that period he was connected with the government of the city, and he was also interested in its institutions of finance and business ; and in the relations thus formed his opinions were much regarded and largely followed.

In 1856 he was appointed Judge of Probate for the County of Middlesex, the county that at that time was the most populous and the most important county in the Commonwealth.

It was then that Judge Richardson became known to the State. In a few years thereafter he received the appointment of Judge of the combined Courts of Probate and Insolvency for the same County.

His services in the two offices covered a period of about sixteen years, and his administration, from beginning to end, was free from criticism or complaint. During that period he was often called to act as referee in important cases, when the parties wished to avoid the delay and expense of litigation in the courts.

In that same period he performed two most important services, one for the State in the revision of its laws, and the other in behalf of good learning in the reformation of the Board of Overseers of Harvard College. He was a member of the Commission that revised the laws of the State as they appeared in the year 1860. I would not be unjust to his associates upon the Commission, but it was the opinion of those who were most carefully instructed upon the subject, that the more delicate and difficult parts of the work were performed by him. To all of us, whether of the Bench or of the Bar, it is known that he was ready at all times in age as in youth to assume any work that was in the line of his duty, or of his profession. He was one of three men, who, graduates of the college, were instrumental in securing a change of the law by which the election of the overseers is vested in the alumni of the college. This change has contributed materially to the prosperity that has attended the college, in these last five and twenty years, under the wise and efficient administration of President Eliot.

It was with great reluctance, and only after long delay and much urging on my part, that Judge Richardson consented to resign his office in Massachusetts and to accept the place of Associate Secretary of the Treasury. His office in Massachusetts was an honorable office, its duties were agreeable to him, he was among his early and long-tried friends, and on every side he was honored and respected.

After a delay of several months he yielded to my importunities, but against his own inclination, and he thus entered a larger field of public service.

In the three and a half years of our association he contributed largely to whatever of success was attained during my administration of the Treasury Department.

I pass over all minor events and incidents, that I may speak of one important service which may not have been paralleled in our history, or in the history of any other country.

In the year 1871, a subscription was made in London for one hundred and thirty-four million of five per cent. United States bonds, the transaction to be consummated in London, the first day of December of that year, and payment to be made in gold, or in five-twenty six per cent. bonds.

Judge Richardson was charged with the duty of making the transfer. He was assisted by a corps of clerks, but the duty and the responsibility were on him. The larger part of the new bonds was paid for by the delivery of old five-twenty bonds, par for par, but the payments in gold ran far up into the millions. The gold funds were invested subsequently in five-twenty bonds at par, and at the end of a few months the Treasury received one hundred and thirty-four million of redeemed five-twenty six per cent. bonds, in exchange for the issue of one hundred and thirty-four million of five per cent. bonds.

The magnitude of this transaction may well make one shudder even after the lapse of a quarter of a century, and so proportionately should be our admiration over the success of its execution. His term of office as Secretary of the Treasury must be measured by months rather than by years, and it was too brief to furnish a full view of his capacity as an executive officer. His administration was marked by a wise, careful attention to business, and by a judicious discharge of every duty.

I have once made this remark in a public way: There is a rough side to Government, and there must be a quality of harshness in those who administer governments successfully. Such generalizations, even if true as rules of action, are subject to exceptions. If it had been the fortune of Judge Richardson to have served on the executive side of the Government for a period of years, and there had been any just cause for criticism, it would have had its origin in the absence of the quality of harshness in his nature.

I count it something—indeed, I count it much in any man's career, that he enjoyed the friendship and confidence of General Grant. That was the good fortune of Judge Richardson to the end of General Grant's life.

General Grant spoke of his friends in a way that distinguished them from other persons. With them he dispensed with all appellations, whether Mr., Colonel or General. In conversations General Sherman was only "Sherman" and Judge Richardson was only "Richardson."

While Judge Richardson held the office of Judge in this Court, and of Chief Justice of the Court, he performed other important work for which his labors in Massachusetts had given him large preparation. The Supplements to the Revised Statutes, which were prepared by him largely and always under his direction, are evidences of his painstaking industry, and of his aptitude rising quite near to genius, for the codification and arrangement and notation of statutes, qualifications not appreciated even by the members of the profession, and by the general public they are not considered, nor even known. If the index of the Revised Statutes of 1878 has ever been criticised, the criticism has not fallen under my notice. Indeed, the statement has been made that one of the States of the Union required the revisers of its statutes to accept as a model the index of the

Revised Statutes of the United States. The plan and the organization of the plan of that index are due to Judge Richardson ; and of the work, especially in the arrangement, a large part was performed by him.

Its volume may be realized from the fact that there are about twenty-five thousand references, and that there are at least three references by substantive words, to every phase of legislative action. His skill in the organization and arrangement of the index may be best seen by reference to the reading under the heading of "Crimes."

The death of Judge Richardson gives me the only opportunity that was possible of placing the honor of the index, which must mean something with the profession, to the credit of his name and memory.

The indulgence of the Court must be asked when I say that it is the misfortune of the Court, now realized in the case of Judge Richardson, that it does not speak in the language which is the language of the courts of the country and of the English world. This Court deals largely with causes arising under statutes which gives the individual a right of action against the United States on claims sounding in contract. It has no jurisdictions over controversies between private parties, it has no common law jurisdiction ; and its equity powers, as granted by recent statutes, are limited, though as yet they have not been fully tested. By the statutes which gave to this Court a qualified jurisdiction over claims known as French Spoliation Claims, questions of international law, and questions touching the value of decisions of foreign courts, were considered by the tribunal, but at the end of an experience of half a century it is to be said that but few of its decisions are applicable as precedents, or as authorities in common law or equity courts.

Hence it has happened that the bar and the judiciary of the country have been ignorant of the doings of this Court ; and hence it is that the late Chief Justice did not acquire the standing as a jurist that he would have reached had he had a seat in a court of general jurisdiction.

These observations should not lead us to undervalue the questions raised and the decisions rendered in this Court. There are but few courts in the country, if indeed there are any, in which the controversies are of more importance, or in which the ascertainment of the facts is more difficult.

As a summary, it is not too much to say that the late Chief Justice met, and fully met, every reqirement that is essential in a judge. In learning he was fully prepared for every exigency of the bar or of the bench ; he was urbane in manner and resolute in his purposes ; he was considerate of the rights of others and firm in the maintenance of the just authority of the Court. In fine, his judicial career is without spot or blemish. It is a great tribute to be able to say, and in truth to say, of an associate whose career is ended, that through a period of more than forty years he occupied important places in the public service, and constantly under the public eye, that he was everywhere and always equal to the duty be-

fore him, that he never erred to the injury of State
or country, and that at the end we are not tempted
to draw the veil of oblivion over any day of his public or private life.

Judge WELDON, on behalf of the Court, responded as follows :

Gentlemen of the Bar : The Court receives the
resolutions and proceedings of the Bar in relation
to the death of the late Chief Justice, as a just and
appropriate tribute to the memory of one whose career is well worthy of the highest appreciation of
public esteem.

Chief Justice Richardson had a most successful
and honorable public career, discharging every responsibility and trust imposed upon him with great
credit to himself, and honor and profit to his country.

In his infancy the lines had fallen to him in the
golden medium between competency and wealth ; he
was not borne down by privations, nor enervated by
the expectancy of hereditary riches ; he did not
encounter the difficulty of want, nor the more
dangerous influence of wealth, which so often blights
the ambition and paralyzes the energy of youth.

At the age of twenty-one he graduated from that
institution, which has been from the earliest days of

this country and is now, the pride and boast of American learning. Nature had endowed him with the highest and best qualifications of the student, lawyer and judge — industry.

In his course at Harvard College he had acquired the ability of close, prolonged and intense mental application, the possession of which enabled him to perform with credit and discharge with success, the many responsibilities which through more than half a century devolved upon him.

Underlying the individual efforts which he made as student, lawyer, executive officer and judge, were the sterling qualities of that character which he had inherited from a long line of ancestry, embodying the characteristics of that noble race which developed New England in all the elements that constitute a great people.

He was highly educated in the perfect discipline of his mind, being enabled, because of such discipline, to bestow upon any subject of investigation the undivided and prolonged thought of his whole being; and that, in the end, is the perfection of education. Education is not necessarily scope and breadth of information; its highest and best quality is the mental aptitude to investigate and understand the complex questions of mind and matter.

Upon his graduation the Chief Justice chose the profession of the law as the vocation of his life; and to its study and practice he brought those habits of trained thought which he had acquired in the discipline of the schools.

Public observation, which is not slow to discern

aptitudes and qualifications fitting men for public trust, soon conferred upon him the confidence of its appreciation in his selection to revise the statutes of Massachusetts, a work which he continued to do for more than twenty years. He was again selected by the legislature to edit the Supplement of the Statutes, which he did to the satisfaction of the legislature, and of a bar, the most critical of any in the United States.

In 1856, he became the Judge of Probate and Insolvency in a county second to only one in the State of Massachusetts. In the discharge of the duties of that important office, he again marked his official career with that ability and industry by which and in which were performed the acts of his whole life, as a guardian of a private or public trust.

In 1869, having declined higher judicial honors in the State of Massachusetts, he became Assistant Secretary of the Treasury, his lifelong and devoted friend, Governor Boutwell, being the Secretary. In that capacity he went to Europe as the financial agent of the United States to adjust and arrange some of the most delicate and important matters connected with the public credit; and on his return he became Secretary of the Treasury. In the discharge of the duties of that high office he infused the spirit of that industry and purity of purpose which in all the relations of life had been the marked individuality of his public and private career.

He was Secretary of the Treasury during the panic of 1873; and by conservative and able counsel, the administration, in the conduct of the Treasury

Department, adhered to and maintained the wise policy of financial integrity.

In 1874, the Chief Justice became, by the appointment of President Grant, a Judge of this Court, in which capacity he served until he became Chief Justice in January, 1885.

His judicial labors on this bench commenced with the tenth and ended with the thirty-first volume of the reports; and it is a melancholy and sad reflection that the opening of the present session marked the boundary of that life which has so richly contributed to the exposition of the law which defines and settles the rights of the citizen and the sovereign.

It is almost useless for me to say to you, Gentlemen of the Bar, that during his labors the litigation of this Court has been very much enlarged, embracing within its scope the decisions of the most complex questions of nearly every branch of the law and the evolution of truth from the widest range of human testimony. For more than twenty-two years, the arduous and responsible duties of a Judge and Chief Justice of this Court were discharged by him with an ability and faithfulness adequate to the full requirement of the positions.

The information which he acquired while Secretary of the Treasury was of great service to the Court in the adjudication of cases involving questions of statutory construction applicable to that department. His mind had great power of retention, and a principle of administrative law was recalled with ready reference when it became applicable in the litigation of the Court.

The twenty-one volumes of the reports in which may be found his opinions on the varied questions of our jurisdiction are a lasting memorial to his name and fame. They will remain as landmarks of the law as long as our system of government endures, and this forum shall be open for the adjudication of national obligations. The good of his life is not "interred with his bones."

During almost the entire period of his services on the Bench, notwithstanding the perplexing and manifold duties of the office of Chief Justice, he performed his portion of the labor incident to all the members of the Court, sharing every responsibility and shrinking from no task, however burdensome.

He was most methodical in the habits of his life as a member of the Court, discharging the minor duties of Chief Justice with the same care and attention that he bestowed upon the higher requirements of the position. In Court, as every member of the Bar will attest, he was as free from judicial tyranny as any judge could be, and administered the power of his high trust in the kindest consideration of all.

The "insolence of office" sometimes manifested in courts of justice found no place in what he said or did in the discharge of his duty in the administration of the office of Chief Justice. Patience, forbearance, courtesy and consideration toward all, marked the lineaments of his official character.

In that beneficent economy of nature which provides aptitudes for the necessities of the race, from the rudest state of society to the highest developments of civilization, the Chief Justice was endowed

with the faculty of justice, which discerns through
the mazes of judicial controversy the substantial
rights of litigants founded upon the fundamental
principles of the laws.

  * * * * For justice
All places a temple, and all seasons summer.

His mind was of the practical and substantial
mold, free from intellectual prejudice, ready to
change when reason dictated, uninfluenced by the
pride of opinion, or the dangerous and unreasonable
demands of consistency.

His opinions are fine specimens of judicial statement, terse in words yet comprehensive in thought,
saying nothing beyond the requirements of the case,
and enunciating the principle of the decision so
clearly that its authority is unquestioned.

In the branch of statutory law, the Chief Justice
had rare qualifications as a Judge. His knowledge
of that department of jurisprudence has not been
excelled in the history of this country. His patient
and unremitting power of investigation, his accurate
and clear conception of legal principles embodied in
the forms of statutory enactment, his varied experience in the revision and construction of acts of the
legislature of his native State, and of the laws of Congress, conferred upon him the highest quality of
ability involving the correct exposition of the law
as founded upon the will of the legislature.

The truth of this statement is abundantly verified
in the many opinions delivered by him in this Court ;
and in the volumes of the Revised Statutes, both State

and National, which bear the imprint of his genius. They are more complimentary to his memory than the praise of a friendship, however fervent.

In 1880, he was selected by joint resolution of Congress to prepare and edit the "Supplement to the Revised Statutes," a work "embracing the statutes general and permanent in their nature, passed after the Revised Statutes, with references connecting the provisions on the same subject, explanatory notes, citations of judicial decisions and a general index."

The work as first published extended from the date the Revised Statutes went into effect (1873) to the adjournment of the Forty-sixth Congress, in 1881. So useful was this work, in bringing together the permanent legislation of general import, segregated from the mass of private and temporary legislation with which it is intermingled in the Statutes-at-Large, that Congress, ten years later, provided for a second edition of the work, bringing it down to date, and including eighteen years of legislation, from 1874 to 1891, and constituting what is known as the "Supplement to the Revised Statutes, Volume 1, Second Edition." In 1893, the work was made a continuing and permanent one, to be prepared at each session of Congress.

During the summer, although wasted in form, broken in health and fully conscious of the near approach of death, he continued his labors with undiminished interest in the preparation of the present volume, surrendering at last to that invincible enemy which in the end conquers us all.

His career was a success, filling as it did the measure of a half century with the fruits of patient and patriotic toil in the public and private relations of life.

The positions which he occupied in the civil service are not surrounded by the glamour of popular applause, but in the conservative virtue of their influence they are most important to the success and the perpetuity of that system of liberty which recognizes equality as the basis of civil and political power.

His valuable labors on the bench, in the field of statutory publications, his services in the executive branch of the government, entitle him to the respect and admiration of the bar and the gratitude of his country.

The Chief Justice has passed into a memory; but what he did remains. Let us hope that his labors, in common with those of the sages of the law, may stand as a safe depository of the rights of individuals, may calm and mitigate the struggles of parties in the coming years of free institutions; and that the voice of judicial reason may conserve and preserve the landmarks of constitutional liberty to the latest period of time.

May our history vindicate the truth that

Virtue alone outbuilds the pyramids,
Her monuments shall last when Egypt's fall.

By order of the Court the request of the Bar is granted, and the Resolutions will be entered of record, to endure as a lasting memorial to the memory of Chief Justice WILLIAM A. RICHARDSON.

The Court thereupon adjourned for the day.

REPORT OF THE METHOD ADOPTED BY ASSISTANT SECRETARY RICHARDSON, AT LONDON, TO KEEP SAFE THE MONEY RECEIVED FROM SALE OF THE FUNDED LOAN.

41 LOMBARD STREET,
LONDON, *Jan'y 25th, 1872.*

Hon. GEORGE S. BOUTWELL,
Secretary of the Treasury.

DEAR SIR:

It is my purpose in this letter to give you an account of the way in which I have kept the money arising from the sale of the Funded Loan, and the manner in which it has been drawn from time to time to pay for bonds purchased and redeemed.

Immediately after the first of December, '71, the money began to accumulate very rapidly. Up to the first of December no money whatever had been received, all bonds delivered having been paid for by the called bonds and coupons, or secured by deposit of other bonds; but on the second day of that month nearly two and a-half millions of dollars cash were paid to me; then, on the 4th, nearly five millions of dollars more; and on the 5th, above three millions, and so on in different sums till the present time. Of course it was wholly impracticable to receive, handle, count and keep on hand such large amounts of gold coin, weighing between a ton and three-quarters and two tons to each million of dollars. At one time my account showed more than sixteen millions of dollars on hand, and to have withdrawn from circulation that amount of coin would have produced a panic in the London market, and the risk in having it hoarded in any place within my reach would have been immense, especially as it would soon have been known where it was.

I ascertained that there would be some difficulty in keeping an official government account in the Bank of England, and I did not feel authorized, or justified on my own judgment, in entrusting so much money to any other Banking Institution in this city. I found also that the Bank of England never issues certificates of deposit, as do our banks in the United States. But it issues "post notes," which are very nearly like its ordinary demand notes, but *payable to order* and on seven days time; thus differing only in the matter of time from certificates of deposit. Availing myself of this custom of the Bank of England, I put all the money into post notes, and locked them up in one of the safes from which the bonds had been taken. This I regarded as a safe method of keeping the funds, and I anticipated no further difficulty.

But when the Bank made its next monthly or weekly return of its condition, and published it in all the newspapers as usual, the attention of all the financial agents, bankers, and financial writers of the daily money articles in the journals was immediately attracted to the sudden increase of the "post

notes'' outstanding, and the unusually large amount
of them, so many times greater than had ever been
known before. They were immensely alarmed lest
the notes should come in for redemption in a few
days, and the coin therefor should be withdrawn
from London and taken to a foreign country; and
lest there should be a panic on account thereof.
Some of the financial writers said they belonged to
Germany, and that they represented coin which
must soon be transmitted to Berlin. The Bank officers themselves, although they knew very well that
these notes belonged to the United States, were not
less alarmed because they feared that I would withdraw the money to send it to New York, which they
knew would make trouble in the London Exchange.
Money, which for a short time before had been at
the high rate of interest, for this place, of five per
cent., had become abundant and the people were
demanding of the Bank a reduction in the rate. But
so timid were they about these post notes that they
did not change the rate till I took measures to allay
their fears. This I did because I thought it would
be injurious and prejudicial to the Funded Loan,
to have a panic in London, in which the market
price of the new loan would drop considerably below
par just at a time when its price and popularity were
gradually rising, and just as it was coming into
great favor with a new class of investors in England,
the immensely rich but timid conservatives.

I determined to open a deposit account with the
Bank of England, and in doing so experienced the
difficulties which I anticipated. I assured the offi-

cers that the money was government (U. S.) money, which I did not intend, and was not instructed, to take home with me; but which I should use in London in redeeming bonds and coupons, and should leave in the Bank on deposit unless by the peculiarity of their rules I should be obliged to withdraw it. They objected to taking the money as a government deposit, or as an official deposit in my name, having some vague idea that if they took it and opened an official government account, they should be liable for the appropriation of the money, unless documents from the United States were filed with them taking away that liability; but they could not tell me exactly what documents they wanted, nor from whom they must come. They did, however, agree to open an account with me, and that was the best I could do. In signing my name to their book I added my official title, and when, some time after, I came to drawing checks I signed in the same way. This brought from the officers a letter, which I annex hereto, saying that my deposit would be regarded as a private and personal one.

What I was most anxious to provide for was the power in some United States officer to draw the money in case of my death, (knowing the uncertainty of life,) without the delay, expense and trouble which must necessarily arise, if it stood wholly to my personal credit. I asked the officers to allow it to stand in your name as Secretary, and mine as Assistant Secretary, jointly and severally, so as to be drawn upon the several check of either, and by the survivor in case of the death of either one. I suggested other arrangements which would have the same result, but they said their rules prevented their agreeing to my requests, that they were conservative and did not like to introduce anything new into their customs.

On the 15th day of January, 1872, I renewed my request in writing, after having had several conversations with the officers on the subject, and received an answer which, with the letter of request, is hereto annexed.

In this, their most recent communication, they express a willingness to enter the account in our joint names as I suggested, regarding it however as a "personal account," and requiring that you should "join in the request and concur in the conditions proposed before either party can in that case draw upon the account."

As I must now almost daily draw from the account for money with which to pay bonds I cannot join your name therein until you have sent me a written compliance with the conditions which they set forth ; because to do so would shut me out from the account altogether for several weeks. Besides, having no instructions from you on the subject, I don't know that you would care to give written directions as to the deposit. I know very well that, in case of my sudden decease, you would be glad enough to find that you could at once avail yourself of the whole amount of money here on deposit, and so I should have joined your name as I have stated.

Now you can do as you please. I have taken every possible precaution within my power, and have no fear that the arrangements are insufficient to protect the Government in any contingency whatever. With the correspondence which has passed between the officers of the Bank and myself, and our conversation together, the account is sufficiently well known to them as a U. S. government deposit, and is fully enough stamped with that character, as I intended it should be, however much they may ignore it now.

But for still greater caution, I made a written declaration of trust on the very day of the first deposit, signed and sealed by me, declaring the money and account as belonging to our Government and not to me, a copy of which is hereto annexed.

I also gave written instructions to Messrs. Bigelow and Prentiss to draw all the checks and how to draw them and keep an account thereof. As I make all my purchases through Jay Cooke, McCullough, & Co., every check is in fact payable to that house, so that the account is easily kept, and the transactions cannot be mingled with others, for there are no others. I annex a copy of these instructions.

This, I believe, will give you a pretty correct idea of the difficulties which have been presented to me in the matter of taking, keeping, and paying out the money arising from the sale of the bonds, and the manner in which I have met them.

I may add that when the officers of the Bank were satisfied that I was not to withdraw the money and take it to New York, they reduced the rate of interest, and there has been an easy money market ever since.

There are now on deposit more than twelve millions

of dollars; but I hope it will be reduced very fast next month. Had you not sent over the last ten millions of bonds, we should have been able to close up very soon. I hope now that you will make another call of twenty millions at least, because I think it would enable us to purchase more rapidly.

I annex :

1. Copy of my declaration of trust.
2. Copy of instructions for drawing checks.
3. Copy of letter from Cashier of Bank of England, stating that the account would be considered personal.
4. Copy of my letter to the Governor of the Bank, asking that your name might be joined.
5. Copy of reply to last mentioned letter.

I am, very respectfully,
Your obedient servant,
WILLIAM A. RICHARDSON.

[COPY]

Whereas I have this day deposited in my name as Assistant Secretary of the Treasury, U. S. A., in the Bank of England, Two Millions five hundred and fifty thousand pounds sterling, and shall probably hereafter make further deposits on the same account.

Now I hereby declare that said account and deposits present and future, are official and belong to the Government of the United States, and not to me personally ; that the monies so deposited are the proceeds of the sale of five per cent. bonds of the " Funded Loan ; " that whatever money I may at any time have in said bank under said account will be the property of the United States Government held by me officially as Assistant Secretary of the Treasury, acting under orders from the Secretary; that the same is, and will continue to be subject to the draft, check, order, and control of the Secretary of the Treasury independently of, and superior to my authority whenever he so elects, and that upon his assuming control thereof my power over the same will wholly cease. In case of my decease before said account is closed the money on deposit will not belong to my estate, but to the Government of the United States.

    Witness my hand and seal.

WILLIAM A. RICHARDSON,

Assistant Secretary of the Treasury, U. S.

LONDON, ENG.   [L. S.]

    December 28, 1871.

Witnesses. { JNO. P. BIGELOW.
              E. W. BOWEN.
              GEO. L. WARREN.

[COPY]

41, LOMBARD ST.

LONDON, ENG., *Dec. 28, 1871.*

To JOHN P. BIGELOW, *Chief of the Loan Division*,

    Secretary's Office, Treasury Department, U. S. A.

    I have this day deposited in the Bank of England in my name as Assistant Secretary of the Treasury, Two Million five hundred and fifty thousand pounds sterling money belonging to the United States, received in payment of five per cent. bonds of the Funded Loan delivered here in London.

All money hereafter received for future delivery of bonds will be deposited to the same account.

Herewith I hand you a declaration of trust signed by me, declaring that said account and monies belong to the United States, and not to me personally, also the deposit book and a book of blank checks numbered from 35101 to 35150, both inclusive, received from said Bank, all of which you will take into your custody and carefully keep in one of the iron safes sent here from the Department, in the same manner as the books are kept.

This money and all the money deposited in said Bank on the account aforesaid, will be drawn and used only in accordance with the orders of the Secretary of the Treasury to redeem or purchase five twenty bonds and matured coupons, or such other and further orders as he may make in relation thereto.

When money is to be drawn to pay for bonds or coupons it must be drawn only by filling up a check from the book of checks above referred to, and you will open an account in which you will enter the amount of all deposits, the number and amount of each check drawn, specifying also to whom the same is made payable and on what account it is drawn.

The checks will be filled up by Mr. Prentiss of the Register's Office, who will place his check mark on the upper left corner, and will enter the same in the book. You will then carefully examine the check, see that it is correctly drawn for the amount actually payable for bonds or coupons received, and properly recorded; and you will when found correct, place your check mark on the right hand upper corner before the same is signed by me. All checks will be signed by me with my full name as Assistant Secretary of the Treasury, as this is signed.

WILLIAM A. RICHARDSON,
Assistant Secretary of the
Treasury, U. S. A.

BANK OF ENGLAND, E. C.
4th Jan'y, 1872.

Hon. W. A. RICHARDSON,
Assistant Secretary of the Treasury
of the United States,
41 Lombard St.

SIR :

To preclude any possible misunderstanding hereafter as to the character of the Drawing account opened in your name, I am instructed by the Governors to communicate to you in writing that, in conformity with the rule of the Bank, the account is considered a personal one; that the Governors have admitted the words appended to your name merely as an honorary designation; and that the Bank take no cognizance of, or responsibility with reference to the real ownership, or intended application of the sums deposited to the credit of the account.

I am,
Sir,
Your obedient Servant,
GEORGE FORBES,
Chief Cashier.

41 LOMBARD ST.
LONDON, ENG.
January 15, 1872.

GEORGE LYALL, Esq.
Governor of the Bank of England.

DEAR SIR:

Referring to the several conversations which I have had with you, and with your principal cashier Mr. Forbes, relative to the manner and form of keeping the account which I desire to have in the Bank, I beg leave to renew in writing my request heretofore made to you orally, that the account of money deposited by me may stand in the name of Hon. George S. Boutwell, Secretary of the Treasury, U. S. A., and myself, Assistant Secretary, jointly and severally, so as to be subject to the several draft of either, and of the survivor, in case of the death of either one.

I suppose I must regard the letter of Mr. Forbes to me, dated January 4, 1872, and written under instructions from the Governors of the Bank as expressing your final conclusion that the account, in whatever form it may be kept, must be considered a personal one.

You know my anxiety to have my deposits received by the Bank and entered in such way that in case of my death, the balance may be drawn at once by the Secretary of the Treasury or some other Officer of the Government, and although you are unwilling to regard the account as an official one, I hope that on further consideration you will allow it to be opened in the name of Mr. Boutwell and myself jointly and severally as above stated.

I am Sir,

Your obe'd't Servant,

WILLIAM A. RICHARDSON,

Assistant Secretary of the

United States Treasury Dept.

[COPY]

BANK OF ENGLAND E. C.

17th January, 1872.

Hon. W. A. RICHARDSON,
    Assistant Secretary of the Treasury
        of the United States,
                41, Lombard St.

SIR :

I am directed by the Governor to acknowledge the receipt of your letter of the 15th inst., requesting that the account of money deposited by you in the Bank may stand in the name of the Hon. George S. Boutwell, Secretary of the Treasury U. S. A., and yourself, the Assistant Secretary, jointly and severally, so as to be subject to the several draft of either, and of the survivor, in case of death of either one.

I am to inform you that the Bank is prepared to open an account in this form, as a personal account; but it is essential that Mr. Boutwell should join in the request, and concur in the conditions proposed, before either party can in that case draw upon the account.　　　I am Sir,

Your Obd't Servant,

GEORGE FORBES,

Chief Cashier.

DEGREES, COMMISSIONS, ETC., HELD BY WILLIAM ADAMS RICHARDSON.

A striking proof of the busy life led by Chief Justice Richardson, is afforded by a glance at the following list of honors conferred on him, of official positions that he from time time held, and of the promotions that he earned.*

It may attract attention that the promotion from a Judge of the Court of Claims to be Chief Justice of that Court was his *fifth* appointment as judge for life, viz.: 1, Judge of Probate for the County of Middlesex, 1856; 2, Judge of Probate and Insolvency for the same County, 1858; 3, Judge of the Superior Court of Massachusetts (declined), 1869; 4, Judge of the United States Court of Claims, 1874; Chief Justice of that Court.

Perhaps in States where the elections are for a short term, a judge may have had five, or even more, commissions; but five life commissions must be rare.

---

*It is proper to say that the list is taken from a rough draft found among the papers of the distinguished Chief Justice. That he should have taken pains to jot down these statistics is eminently characteristic of the man. He liked (in fact it was almost a passion with him) to arrange and classify, and to present in clear and intelligible form, the "upshot of the whole matter."

COLLEGIATE.

1843. Bachelor of Arts.   Harvard College.
1846. Bachelor of Laws.   "   "
      Master of Arts.   "   "
1873. Doctor of Laws.   Columbia University, D. C.
1881.   "   "   "   Georgetown College, D. C.
1882.   "   "   "   Howard University, D. C.
1886.   "   "   "   Dartmouth College.

LAW.

1846. Admission to Bar in Massachusetts.
1869. Admission to Bar, Supreme Court U. S.
1855. Commission to revise the Statutes of Massa-
      chusetts.
1859. Act of Legislature of Mass., appointing com-
      missioners to edit the General Statutes.
1866. Commission as to laws authorizing formation
      of corporations with limited liabilities.
1870. Commission concerning Hingham and Quincy
      Turnpike and Bridges.
1880. Act of Congress authorized editing and pub-
      lishing a Supplement to the Revised Stat-
      utes of the United States.
1882. Appointment to edit Vol. 18, Court of Claims
      Reports.
1890. Act of Congress continuing publication of Sup-
      plement to Revised Statutes.
1893. Act of Congress continuing same annually.

POLITICAL.

1849. Member of Common Council, Lowell, Mass.

1852. Member and President of Common Council, Lowell, Mass.

1853. Member and President of Common Council, Lowell, Mass.

1869. Assistant Secretary of the Treasury (U. S.)

Acting Secretary, April 23, 1869, in absence of Secretary.

Acting Secretary, June 8, 1869, until otherwise ordered.

Acting Secretary, April 16, 1869, until otherwise ordered.

1870. Acting Attorney-General, Sept. 8, 1870.

1873. Secretary of the Treasury (U. S.)

JUDICIAL. (ALL FOR LIFE.)

1856. Judge of Probate for Middlesex County, Mass. Last to hold the office.

1858. Judge of Probate and Insolvency for Middlesex County, Mass. First to hold the office.

1869. Associate Justice Superior Court of Massachusetts (declined).

1873. Judge of Court of Claims (U. S.)

1885. Chief Justice Court of Claims (U. S.)

JUSTICE OF PEACE, ETC.

1847. Justice of the Peace for Middlesex County, Mass., for seven years.

1853. Notary Public for Middlesex County, Mass., for seven years.

1854. Justice of the Peace for Middlesex County, Mass., for seven years.

1856. Justice of Peace and Quorum within all the counties of Massachusetts for seven years.
1863. Same.
1870. "
1877. "

MILITIA OF MASSACHUSETTS.

1846. Judge Advocate of Second Division with rank of Major.
1850. Aid de Camp to the Commander in Chief with the rank of Lieutenant Colonel.

SOCIETIES, ETC.

1852. Member of Middlesex Mechanics Association, Lowell, Mass.
1857. Member of New England Historic Genealogical Society, Boston, Mass.
1863. Trustee of Lawrence Academy (Groton, Mass.)
1872. Member of Washington National Monument Association (Washington, D. C.)
1873. Honorary Vice-President of New England Historic Genealogical Society.
Honorary Member of Middlesex Mechanics Association, Lowell, Mass.
1874. Honorary Member of Nashua Historical Society, Nashua, New Hampshire.
Trustee of Howard University, Washington, D. C.
1881. Trustee of All Souls Church, Washington, for three years.
1886. Trustee of All Souls Church, Washington, for three years.

1886. Fellow of American Geographical Society.

1879. Member of Royal Historical Society (London, Eng.)

1880. Member of Society of Antiquities (Edinburgh, Scotland.)

Honorary Member of New Hampshire Historical Society.

1889. Corresponding member of Maine Historical Society.

1890. Honorary and Corresponding Member of Old Residents' Historical Association (Lowell, Mass.)

1891. Member of Society of the Sons of the American Revolution (D. C.)

Member of Society of Sons of the Revolution (Mass.)

1893. Honorary Member of New England Historic Genealogical Society.

MISCELLANEOUS.

1863. Overseer of Harvard College, elected for six years by Legislature of Massachusetts.

1869. Overseer of Harvard College, elected by the Alumni for six years.

1883. Commission to test and examine the fineness and weight of coin at the several mints, appointed by President Arthur.

Of many other appointments, such as Prof. of Law in Georgetown University, President of Bank, Director in Banks and Manufacturing Companies, etc., notice was given orally only.

MASONIC.

1853. Member of Ancient York Lodge, Lowell, Mass.

1857. Member of Mount Horeb, Royal Arch Chapter, Lowell, Mass.

Member of Boston Encampment of Knights Templar, Boston, Mass.

1866. Sovereign Grand Inspector General of the 33d Degree, etc., etc.

1882. Commission of enquiry into the condition of Masonic Order abroad from Superior Council of Sovereign Grand Inspectors General of the 33d and last degree, of Northern Masonic Jurisdiction (U. S.)

PASSPORTS, ETC.

1865. Passports with numerous "vises."

1867.   "   "   "   "

1871.   "   as Assistant Secretary of the Treasury.

"   "   Bearer of Dispatches.

1875.   "   "   Judge of Court of Claims with letter of introduction from President Grant.

Japanese passport to travel in interior of the country (with various documents relating to the journey).

1890. Passport as Chief Justice Court of Claims, with letter of introduction from Secretary Blaine.

1865. Circular letter in Latin from Bishop of Boston. Letter of presentation to the Pope.

1882. Circular letter to Historical Societies from New England Hist. Genealogical Society, Boston.

A PARTIAL BIBLIOGRAPHY OF THE PUBLISHED WRITINGS OF WILLIAM ADAMS RICHARDSON.

I. Banking Laws of Massachusetts : Being a compilation of all the General Statutes of the Commonwealth, now in force, relating to banks, banking and savings institutions, with notes, references to alterations in the statutes, abstracts of decisions of the Supreme Judicial Court and quotations from reports of the bank commissioners. By William A. Richardson, counsellor at law. Lowell : Merritt & Metcalf; Boston : Sanborn, Carter & Bazin. 1855. 8vo. pp. 82.

II. Practical Information Concerning the Public Debt of the United States with the National Banking Laws for Banks, Bankers, Brokers, Bank Directors and Investors. By William A. Richardson, Assistant Secretary of the Treasury. Washington, D. C.: W. H. and O. H. Morrison, Law Publishers and Booksellers. 1872. 8vo. pp. 186. [Second edi-•tion was published in 1873.]

III. Annual Report of the State of the Finances to the Forty-Third Congress, First Session, December 1, 1873, by William A. Richardson, Secretary of the Treasury. Washington : Government Printing Office. 1873. pp. xxxix.

IV. Letter, December 23, 1881, to Hon. John Sherman, United States Senator, in relation to the best method of determining controverted questions in customs-revenue cases. Washington, 1881. pp. 5.

V. Trials in Customs-Revenue Cases. No date. pp. 6.

Note.—This was written by William A. Richardson and adopted by Mr. Lawrence, First Comptroller of the Treasury.

VI. Receipt and Investment of the Geneva Award Money. Letter of William A. Richardson, June 22, 1882. pp. 7. Reprinted from The Geneva Award Act, with notes and references to Decisions of the Court of Commissioners of Alabama Claims, by Frank W. Hackett, of the Washington (D. C.) Bar. Boston : Little, Brown, & Company. 1882.

VII. History, Jurisdiction and Practice of the Court of Claims (United States) by William A. Richardson, LL.D., Chief Justice of the Court. Washington: Government Printing Office. 1883. pp. 34. Second Edition, June, 1885.

VIII. Harvard College. Class of 1843. Memorabilia. 1883. "Time comes stealing on by night and day." *Shakespeare.* Prepared by William A. Richardson, Class Secretary. Printed for the use of the Class, June 27, 1883. pp. 37.

IX. Harvard College Alumni who have held the Official Positions named. By William A. Richardson, LL.D., Chief Justice of Court of Claims (U. S.) Washington, D. C. Reprinted from the New England Historical and Genealogical Register for July, 1887. pp. 7.

X. Report of Special Committee, on the Relief of Congress from Private Legislation, to the American Bar Association at its Tenth Annual Meeting, at Saratoga Springs, New York, August, 1887. (Reprinted from the transactions of the Meeting.) Philadelphia : T. & J. W. Johnson & Co. 1887. pp. 12.

Note.—On the copy found among the papers of the Chief Justice, in his handwriting, is inscribed :

"Written for the Committee by W. A. R., who also wrote the original Senate Bill. But what is erased on page 6 was not by W. A. R., but was interlined after he wrote the report, and is erroneous." The words erased are: "also of all damages by vessels of the United States done by collision."

XI. Harvard College Alumni who have received the Honorary Degrees named. By the Hon. William A. Richardson, LL.D., Chief Justice of the Court of Claims, Washington, D. C. Reprinted from the New England Historical and Genealogical Register for April, 1889. pp. 12.

XII. Chief Justice of the United States, or Chief Justice of the Supreme Court of the United States? By the Hon. William A. Richardson, LL.D., Chief Justice of the Court of Claims, Washington, D. C. The New England Historical and Genealogical Register, for July, 1895. pp. 4.

XIII. Harvard University. College Presidents and the Election of Messrs. Quincy and Eliot. By the Hon. Wm. A. Richardson, (H. U., 1843) LL.D., Chief Justice Court of Claims. University Magazine, Dec., 1891. Reprinted in the New England Historical and Genealogical Register for January, 1895. pp. 6.

*₊*The list, it will be seen, does not include (1) Report as Commissioner to revise the Statutes of Massachusetts; (2) Notes, etc., to General Statutes of that State, 1860; (3) Notes, etc., in twenty-two annual volumes of Statutes of Massachusetts; (4) Notes, etc., to Supplements to the Revised Statutes of the United States.

INDEX OF NAMES

INDEX OF NAMES.

_____

Roman Numerals Refer to Pages of the APPENDIX.

3

7

8